The Fantastical Adventures

of

Dottie Moorehead

The Fantastical Adventures of Dottie Moorehead

By

R. L. Holland

Small House Publishing
Ireland
smallhousepublishing@gmail.com

ISBN 978-1-5272-8261-2
First edition, 2020

Edited by Katie Ahern
Cover Illustration and cover design by Claudia McKinney
© 2020 Phatpuppyart.

The Fantastical Adventures of Dottie Moorehead is
dedicated to:

The Fantastical Ger, Rosie, Harry, Minnie, Eileen, Michael,
Mary, and George

CONTENTS

CHAPTER 1

Adventurer Extraordinaire

I f Dottie Moorehead wasn't out exploring the woods surrounding her home, on inclement days, she was indoors making use of an antique serving tray to expedite her descent down the old Georgian staircase. She had become so proficient at stair sliding that she could travel at great speed without having any mishaps at all. In her mind's eye she saw herself as this trail-blazing young girl trumping all comers at the Cresta Run or even representing her country one day by becoming the first female Winter Olympian to win a gold medal for the toboggan.

"Come on Dottie, you can do it, you can do it!" she would shout out trying to beat her previous times. Then, looking at the moon-phase grandfather clock in the hallway, she would watch the second-hand edge closer and closer to twelve. With only ten seconds to go she quickly pulled an old, battered pair of motor cyclist's goggles over her eyes, then counted down aloud, "THREE…TWO…ONE…GOOOO!" A tremendous kerfuffle would ensue as Dottie whizzed down the stairs, clattering, and bashing as the tray slipped and skipped over the stair treads. She held on tight to the tray's handles and believed she could control the direction of the runaway tray by sheer willpower. When she landed at the bottom with an almighty crash, she slid to a halt on the highly polished parquet hall floor, and craned her neck, checking the clock to see if she had broken her previous record. She was fearless and very well practiced in the sport, she christened it, The Carpet Cresta Run where she was crowned, by herself of course, perpetual champion for this and any other century, never bested – ever. However, her dedication to her training had its consequences, as she had begun to wear down the centre of the carpet stairs and the patience of her grandmother.

"That's my best tea tray, how could you have such little regard for it? I forbid you from using it again. Do you hear me now Madam?"

"But…. but…. Gran, I was just playing with it," she replied, her head bowed, fidgeting with the blue and orange buttons on her lime green dress, while stubbing the toe of her Mary Jane's into the floor. The disappointment showed on Dottie's face, that dimpled smile was gone, and tears started welling up in her big brown eyes at this immediate ban.

"Don't give me any of your cheek now my girl, do you hear me?"

"Yes, Gran, I hear you, I'm not half deaf…like you," Dottie mumbled under her breath.

"WHAT did you say?" snapped her grandmother.

"Nothing Gran, nothing…" she knew there was no point in arguing with her grandmother; once Granny said 'no' she meant it.

Dottie's grandmother was a stout, low–sized, woman; she walked slowly and stiffly, with a pained expression on her face. She would inhale sharply with each movement as she walked, "Oh, my poor back," she would lament. She had suffered from a motorcycle injury for years, a painful memento of her own youth. Her grey hair was worn in a tight bun at the back of her head. As a widow of her time, she only ever wore black; her skirts all seemed to come from the Victorian era, both in pattern and design. She had her favourite grandchild, Dottie's older sister Viola, she felt that Dottie was always trying her patience and far too chatty a child for her liking. She believed in the dictum; *children should be seen and not heard* so she and Dottie were always destined to clash.

"Now, get up those stairs, sharpish mind, and wash your hands before your tea. Do you hear me Madam?" Her grandmother looked on, the silver tray now back in her possession, a little battered, dented, and worn smooth from its time as a toboggan. Dottie turned back as she slowly climbed the stairs, hoping to entreat her grandmother for a reprieve but it was to no avail, she tried to speak,

"But…but Gran…" all she saw at the end of the stairs was her grandmother waving a finger of disapproval and tut-tutting at a crestfallen Dottie. She turned onto the landing at the top of the stairs, sniffling a little, and then was out of sight. Thus, was the nascent career of this feisty tobogganist cut short before it had even begun.

CHAPTER 2

Muthikos

Dottie was born and reared on Mount Garra Farm in the verdant countryside of Ireland by her parents, her grandmother, and a kindly neighbour and guardian, Nell McGerathy. She spent carefree days roaming the unspoilt, rural landscape where she developed a lifelong appreciation of its flora and fauna. Her father, Henry Moorehead, a Professor of Art History at the university, was an erudite man. In his career he had published countless papers on monuments, specialising in the sculpture of ancient Greece. He had spent his early life travelling to distant lands on an obsession, searching for any traces of the Statue of Zeus at Olympia, and Phidias's Athena Parthenos in the Parthenon, Athens. Both colossal statues are believed to be completely lost, but Dottie's father hoped there might still be tangible evidence of their existence. His work crossed from history and, at times, over into archaeology, which was where he met a zealous doctoral student on a dig in Greece, who was to become his wife and Dottie's mother, Miss Veronica Holland, and the rest, as Dottie's father liked to quip, was art history. As well as being an accomplished academic he had also become a distinguished gentleman farmer, shrewdly appointing a farm manager, Bill Honeycomb, to run the farm in his absences while he was working at the university or on his many research trips abroad. Dottie was indulged by her father as she was his little pet, he doted on her, and when he was home, they spent long, happy days together.

Dottie would do what she could, in her own little way, to help
her father on the farm and in return he would tell her all the
wondrous stories of his travels. He was tall and had a fine head
of hair greying slightly at the temples. He was a kind man,
dashing, charismatic, and had a hint of the Hollywood matinee
idol about him.

After Dottie's parents were married, they did not give up their
love of travelling and bought *Muthikos,* a sailboat, as a honey-
moon present to each other. Both had been keen sailors in
their youth, so they kept up this pursuit, spending the first few
years of married life sailing to faraway places and bringing back
great trinkets from their explorations. Henry was sponsored to
collect artefacts to add to the university's collection, building
up their exhibits of significant relics from around the globe.
On his return to the university lecture hall Dottie's father
brought his subject matter to life. His students got to experience what it was really like to be there when the pharaoh's
tomb was discovered and opened by Carter for the first time.
They got to feel the sense of awe when the treasures entombed
for thousands of years once again came back into view. He
could describe the misty quality of light when the dawn broke
over the River Nile, or the sunset behind the Great Pyramid of
Giza, in a way that had his audience enraptured. His passion
for his subject, and his countless adventures abroad became
theirs; such was his skill and his enthusiasm. In his lectures he
fascinated students with tales of his travels making him the
most popular lecturer at the college. He regaled his classes with
stories of his wondrous voyages; the places he had seen, the
people he had met, their customs and traditions, even sharing
tales of the wild nightlife and colourful characters he had met
once the sun went down. In fact, most students would recall
his classes as if they had attended a dramatic performance at
the theatre rather than a lecture. His unorthodox methods of
teaching were frowned upon at the time by all the more

conservative professors in his department, and yet, much to the more orthodox academicians' irritation, come examination time, all his classes excelled. But while Henry enjoyed lecturing and imparting knowledge onto his students, Dottie's father's first love, and her mother's also, was to sail the ocean on their wonderful Muthikos. Before Viola and Dottie arrived, they had sailed halfway around the globe and still, when they could, they kept that vessel seaworthy and ready for their next great adventure. Dottie would ask her father endlessly about the sights he had seen; about the whales and dolphins off the coast of Morocco surfing the bow wave of Muthikos or of the fascinating people they met when they docked for supplies on far off distant shores. All these tales further ignited her imagination and her father never tired of answering her questions about these mysterious places or forgot to bring back mementos of his adventures for her and her sister. Although he made every effort not to appear to favour one child over the other, Viola was jealous of their close connection; she could tell Dottie shared her father's sense of adventure as well as his curiosity and doughty spirit. Once, when Dottie was just that little bit too young to go sailing with her parents, Viola was taken on the family's yacht to earn her sea legs and help crew the vessel. She felt great pleasure at having both parents all to herself while at sea; her pleasure was multiplied by the fact that for the duration Dottie was stuck at home with their grandmother. The smirk on her face was obvious to all and, but for a rather large seagull who decided to cover her head with his unsavoury business while on deck, she might well have still been smirking after they had docked and driven the long road back home. Instead, she suffered the ignominy of that seagull's blatant attack. Afterwards, the bird appeared to cackle with mirth on his perch in the riggings, seeming to delight in having caused such unpleasantness. "That beast!" Viola glowered at the bird. Even an hour later she was still fuming as her mother washed her hair and her father comforted her from behind his newspaper. Viola could not be certain, but wondered, through narrowed eyes, whether, or not she heard her parents stifle a giggle or two – but perhaps she was mistaken.

CHAPTER 3

Sisters at School

Viola was a dispassionate girl and the very antithesis of Dottie. She was a self-centred and distant human being who, somehow, was never nearby when Dottie was in the mood to play. Instead, little Dottie had to invent her own ways of amusing herself on a regular basis. The two could not have been less alike; chalk and cheese had more in common than Dottie and her elder sibling. When Dottie was sent to school at an early age, her mother said it was to keep Viola company and so as she would not get lonely. This made no sense at all to little Dottie as Viola mostly kept to herself and seemed to get irked whenever Dottie tried to play or chat with her. Even as a small child, Dottie knew where she wanted to be, and once she had surveyed her new surroundings at school on that very first morning, keen to know every nook and cranny of the building, she quickly became bored of it and longed to be back outside in nature. She could not understand why she was being wrenched from her perfect little world of playing, learning, and exploring at home on the farm for the stiff and controlled environment of school. She asked her parents why they made her go to this awful "school place" to learn as she was already learning all she needed from being out in the garden with nature and in the surrounding woods. Her parents would remind her that she needed to learn her ABCs and 123s and that it was good for her. Out of sight of her parents Viola would tell her,

"It's because you're so stupid that they had to try and help you before you became even more stupider to ever learn anything – ever." When Dottie would ask Viola why she would say such mean things, her elder sister would always reply,

"Because that's why!" This answer just frustrated Dottie, later in life she would realise that was Viola's intention.

Every morning Dottie would plead with her mother not to send her away from her beloved home life, but her mother would be unmoved.

"Come along now Dottie, you are getting into that car whether you like it or not, and you are going to school. Do you hear me?" she would say firmly. "Now stop scampering about child, come here right now," her mother would yell as her little daughter would run around the front lawn to try and escape her clutches. Her plan every morning, without fail, would always be the same since she had been fooled that first morning, thinking she would be going to that dreary place for only that one day. But to do THIS every day…. forever…now that was unconscionable. Some mornings if she was caught too quickly, she would just stamp her feet, repeatedly while uttering the words,

"No! No! No! No!" with each stomp. On summer nights the Dean would hang a sheet in the town's square and show movies to raise the townsfolks' spirits. Dottie had been half-asleep in her father's arms but had seen snippets of movies where the plucky P.O.W.s would run a campaign of mass disobedience until the prison guards had to capitulate. These actions had stuck in her mind, so she intended to never make the process of going to school an easy one; resist, resist, resist. But in the end, she would just sit in the back of her father's mauve coloured Ford Model A, arms folded, resigned to her fate. The school building itself was unappealing to her; the grey stone walls, the black, cast-iron radiators, which promised heat yet never seemed to be on (except on days when parents were

invited to visit), it all felt like a prison to Dottie. She hated
every part of that horrible little place and even calling to mind
the hallway where all the small children hung up their little
coats and little hats over ornate wrought iron coat hooks on all
those very early frosty mornings, made her shudder.

"This is horrible," Dottie would think. She cried and cried
knowing she had to separate from her father and spend the
long, long, day in this dusty old room with strange grown-ups
keeping an eye on her and setting rules about how much time
she could have playing with the school's toys. Playing with
them was the only bright part of the day but they remained
locked away for most of the morning or so it seemed to Dottie. Viola would laugh and laugh at her little sister's protests and
was never there to comfort her little sister or support her if she
got frightened by her new surroundings. Structure and routine
matched Viola's personality and she wanted to be part of that
structure. She never much cared for trees and bugs and bees
like Dottie, for she liked learning by rote. This is why she never
shared her sister's passion for her natural surroundings. In
many ways; Viola had more in common with her mother than
Dottie.

CHAPTER 4

Making Do

Their mother was a sophisticated lady, sociable and well educated; she had a doctorate in archaeology but was also engaged with modernity. She could wear anything she liked and make it look stylish and à la mode. She worked tirelessly with the Country Woman's Association, who all remembered rationing from the last Great War, and some argued that shortages were far worse after wartime than during it, so people became accustomed to making do. They lived in fear of the rising tensions in Europe and the increasingly threatening proclamations from abroad on the radio. So, they always felt they needed to be on a war-footing, just in case. She had been reared by a very thrifty mother and so she shared that trait. Because of her life experience, and her own mother's influence, Dottie's mother, when time allowed, loved making jams, treats and tarts, so nothing would ever go to waste; she never liked any waste of any kind, although she could afford to buy new, she preferred to mend and sew. Frugality stayed with her for life and this approach was handed down from one generation to the next. It was this spirit that led Dottie into using her imagination when it came to finding anything sweet tasting to eat, increasing her interest in the food and flowers growing out in the wild. All that could be foraged for was gathered by the household.

"Necessity is the mother of invention," her mother would always say, and the young Dottie took heed.

When they went away exploring and sailing the oceans blue, Dottie's grandmother was left in charge of running the farm with Bill, she ruled with an iron fist and was regarded as a tough woman by all who worked on the farm. There was also the gardener, known only as Molloy, who kept the walled garden in fruit and vegetables all year 'round. The farm might have been run by Dottie's parents, or, at times, by Bill and Grandmother, but the walled garden was different, that was Molloy's domain. Of course, Dottie missed her parents greatly when they were on one of their excursions abroad but would distract herself spending her time exploring the woods and farmlands around her home. She was always trying to outsmart her grandmother to get some sweet treats from the kitchen when she wasn't looking. Her grandmother could not always keep an eye on her feral little granddaughter, but she never worried about her either, as she knew Dottie was out there somewhere and somehow always made it home in time for her tea.

Dottie's grandmother had lived through some very lean times, especially during the First World War, so if there was an abundance one year, then anything that could be stored for the winter months was carefully preserved, canned, or pickled, and so her grandmother seemed to spend the majority of her life in the kitchen. When Dottie's mother was away on business with her father, it was Grandmother who ruled the kitchen, and more particularly, the larder. She was endlessly concocting recipes, and baking a wondrous array of cakes and treats, jellies and jams, pickles and chutneys for the various church fetes and charity drives presided over by the head of their parish, Dean Martin. She was always trying to please the Dean as she had rather a soft spot for him, he would often call over to the house and many a time Dottie would find him being offered some sugar in his tea, which perplexed her, as she was never allowed any in hers. Dean Martin was a plump, elderly man, a widower, with a wispy bit of hair strategically combed over to the other side of his head; kept in place by some carefully applied pomade. He was of low stature, much like her grandmother, but unlike her, had a kind and jolly disposition. He could fill the kitchen with his laughter, and he was the only one who had the key to unlock her grandmother's smile, and on occasion, even a giggle or two from the taciturn old lady. He always brought some homemade chocolate confections for the children when he would call on her, it was because of these that Dottie always forgave the sugar favouritism extended to him by her grandmother, especially as he would put raisins and cherries in his chocolate treats, which she adored.

CHAPTER 5

Turkey Terror

Dottie had dark brown hair down to her shoulders and a thick fringe that was kept cut straight across. Once every few weeks, her grandmother would order Dottie to take a seat from the kitchen table and place it in the centre of the tiled floor. The old lady would rummage around in the drawers of the kitchen press then walk towards Dottie wielding a large pair of tailor's scissors and tell her to sit still. It seemed to be an obsession of hers to keep Dottie's fringe well-trimmed and to keep it out of her eyes,

"Oh, sit STILL, why can't you? If you would just sit still girl, it won't be for much longer, now stop your fidgeting and wriggling," said her grandmother in annoyance. She held Dottie's head up to cut the fringe.

"It's just so itchy, Gran, and it tickles my nose too," said Dottie impatiently, twitching her nose while trying to wriggle down from the chair. Once she was released from her grandmother's hold she bolted from the seat and straight outdoors.

As their parents were away a large amount of the time from the house, Dottie had to find her own ways of entertaining and engaging her boundless curiosity and thirst for knowledge. Invariably, this led Dottie into some sort of mischief or other. She was very much left to her own devices but on one occasion her mother, in an effort to teach her daughters a sense of responsibility, and also, to keep her youngest one out of trouble, gave both girls a clutch of eggs each to hatch. She had borrowed large incubator boxes from the university's agricultural department.

"Now, Dottie," she said, "this is a big responsibility, so I want you to mind these eggs very carefully and make sure they're kept nice and warm. They must be checked, and turned, once every day, you'll remember now, won't you?" wagging her finger playfully at her mischievous little child.

"Oh, do I have to Mummy? I'm far too busy now, I've a lot of other things to do, I'm really, really, busy at the moment. Why can't Viola do it since she has other eggs to hatch anyway?"

"Tut, tut, now Dottie, sisters share the workload, I won't ask you again, I'm trusting you to do your best for me." This was her mother's canny way of diverting Dottie's energy and teaching her responsibility.

"Oh, ok, ok, OK, I suppose I'll have to do it then, won't I?" Dottie said reluctantly.

"Once they're hatched, these chicks will come to depend on you, so I'm trusting you to keep them all fed and watered," her mother put great emphasis on the words 'trusting you,' gently placing her hands on her young daughter's shoulders as if to underscore the import of this task; the burden of responsibility placed on her.

"Ohhh great, more work, and at my age too, I can't wait, what could possibly be better than playing?" thought Dottie sarcastically. After a few weeks, and much to Dottie's dismay, her eggs hatched out, but they were all white, bluish, and featherless little turkey chicks while her sisters were these beautiful fluffy, rusty yellow, little chicks, and one extra cute little chick was pure black in colour. Dottie thought how typical it was that Viola always got the best of everything; just like she got new clothes, new shoes, new toys, she was always first to get everything while Dottie was always given her cast offs. It just felt so unfair. Both girls were given different outhouses in which to rear the birds and Dottie watched hers grow into black feathered turkeys with red heads, while her sister's little chicks grew up into fine Rhode Island Red chickens. One little black chick grew into a pure black chicken with shiny greenish blue-black feathers; this was Viola's favourite which she used to carry everywhere with her, tucked under her arm. Dottie spent quite a lot of her time rearing her birds and she felt like she had developed a strong bond with them. They regarded her as their mother and were very protective of her; all the turkeys grew big and healthy under her care and in a few short months were all as tall as Dottie too. She grew to love those scrappy-looking birds and gave each one of them a name. Dottie also noted their individual personalities; Daisy was feisty, Dora was shy, Patty had a wobbly walk, and Nora liked to perch on her lap. With each new day, she would notice how their personalities developed. One afternoon, Viola walked into the pen where Dottie had been keeping the young turkeys, she was shouting at the top of her voice at Dottie and accusing her, wrongly of course, of having used her favourite hairbrush. The turkeys got a terrible fright and thought their adopted mother was under attack, so they chased her sister around the enclosure till she ran from the pen screaming in fear of them, getting a few painful pecks on her backside as she made good her escape. Dottie tried to calm the birds down and she tried not to laugh at the event she had just witnessed unfold before her very eyes.

Her sister screamed back accusations at Dottie, saying that she made them do it on purpose, she was sure of it.

"I didn't do anything at all, Viola," she proclaimed, but her sister would not hear any of it and continued her tirade.

"You've trained those horrid birds to do that to me on purpose, you horrible, horrible thing, you're just jealous of my chickens," sobbed a disconsolate Viola. "Anyway, your turkeys are ugly just like you Dottie, I hate you, I HATE you!" she cried, tears welling in her eyes.

"Why would I do that to you, you're my *sister*?" Dottie yelled. "Well, I wish you *weren't* my sister," Viola hissed, "I couldn't care less if you were alive or dead," she said sobbing and clutching her sore bottom. "I'm going to tell Gran on you," she roared, "I hate you, I hate, hate, *hate* you," she screamed again, as she ran as fast as she could into the distance back towards the courtyard and around the side entrance to the kitchen. Dottie was feeling quite upset by her sister's cruel remarks, she knew once again that Viola had got it wrong about her using the brush and also, anyone who had a heart could see how beautiful her turkeys were. Dottie laughed whenever she recalled that moment, but it was also tinged with a certain melancholy; as it brought to mind that crisp November morning late in the month when all her beautiful turkeys disappeared, try as she might, she could not find them anywhere, before heading to school. Later that day Dottie asked her mother and father if they had seen her birds, her parents just exchanged sheepish looks at each other and explained to Dottie that her charges had taken flight, gone away somewhere warm for Christmas, and had decided to stay there for good. Although Dottie was heartbroken at the loss of her feathered friends, it was bittersweet, as she was pleased that they had found somewhere pleasant to live and out of the cold, damp winter in Ireland. At least, she thought, Viola's pet hen, Clucky, was staying around and Dottie would be able to play with her instead. Soon, she realised Clucky was not a hen at all, but in fact, a cockerel, and was quite the cross little bird indeed, not at all a suitable playmate for her.

"He must take after Viola," she thought."

CHAPTER 6

Raider of the Larder

Dottie never liked keeping track of time, before the school year began, she never needed to as her days were spent carefree; each one filled with the potential for endless adventures. Her main task, beyond finding some mischief or other to keep entertained each day, was to procure some sweet treats, and the target of her attention was always the larder.

"You'll ruin your tea, so don't even think about it, I'm warning you mind," her grandmother used to say, with a sharp eye on her when she spoke. Much to Dottie's chagrin, her grandmother was forever in the kitchen, apron on, acting as a sentinel standing in the way of Dottie and that well-stocked larder. Her father had once taken her to watch a movie; the Dean had arranged for a screen to be erected in the community hall and there Dottie watched the heroic endeavours of plucky war heroes. She remembered how in the movies the daring soldiers would plan their missions; sometimes having to observe the routines of prison guards when planning their escape, timing each patrol and knowing exactly when to make their heart-stopping break for freedom. Dottie learned fast and would bide her time and watch for when her grandmother's back was turned, knowing that this was when her mind was preoccupied. Dottie would then climb up onto the kitchen countertop unnoticed, open one of the glass door presses to rescue some of the sugar stored within. Her plan was to cut a slice of the still-warm, freshly baked, brown soda bread resting on the kitchen table, slather it with butter and then sprinkle the sugar all over the top. It was calling out to her, wafting that lovely freshly-baked aroma, she managed to cut it, butter it, and have the sugar sprinkled on it before her grandmother turned around, saw what was unfolding, and then tried to stop her.

"DOTTIE! Come back here you cheeky little rascal, do you hear me? There's a wicked streak in you. Do you hear me?! Just wait till I tell your mother, come back here now this instant, I said!" But by then Dottie had the bounty in her hand and was out the door, giggling, on hearing her grandmother's annoyance echoing off in the distance.

CHAPTER 7

Magical Beginnings

S he ran up to the top field into the woods and once there, she sat on her favourite tree stump and prepared to scoff the lot. "Hey, you there, what are you eating?" Dottie looked all around but could not see anyone at all. She responded anyway,

"B..b...brown bread with sugar and butter," Dottie replied a little nervously while still looking all around her.

"I'm down here and I shall have a piece of that, if you don't mind," the voice hollered back. As Dottie looked down, she could just make out a tiny little person standing on a mossy grey rock. There she was looking back at Dottie with translucent wings outstretched as if about to fly upwards.

"Well, I think I only have enough for myself, but maybe you can have a little, Oh, my goodness, you have wings!" Dottie whispered in amazement.

"Of course, I have wings, we all have wings, we are winged folk, so now let's be having some of that bread," her hands held out awaiting a piece of the bounty.

"You're – a – are you a – are you a fairy, aren't you?" Dottie asked trying not to appear totally shocked on witnessing this amazing little person. She was about five inches tall and had a beautiful head of red hair, thick and glossy, and wavy down to her waist, her wings were of a diaphanous light blue shade, and she was wearing the most delicate of dresses with all colours and shades of pink and green, her shoes sparkled like diamonds in the dappled sunlight streaming down on them through the trees, as she fluttered suddenly around Dottie's head,

"Of course, I am a fairy, don't look so surprised, we've been around a lot longer than you guys. Before you were here, WE were. Who'd ya think helped you to discover fire? The Wheel? Mathematics...fairies!" Dottie was a bit flabbergasted as her father and mother had never mentioned the fairies' involvement of any of these pinnacles of human achievement. "Do you know who invented the electric light?" quizzed the fairy.

"Thomas Edison!" replied Dottie; proud she had learned this fact from her father.

"Nope, FAIR-IES" the fairy declared in a sing-song fashion.

"The telephone?" Mabel asked. "Bell!" answered Dottie, "Mr Bell," once more delighted she also knew the correct answer to this question also.

"Not Mr Bell," said the fairy, "his name was Mr BLUEbell and also a.......FAIR-Y!" Then the tiny fairy started giggling; it was hard to know exactly when she was telling the truth and when she was joking, as fairies love a good joke and were forever making up tall tales....despite their diminutive size.

"What's your name?" asked Dottie. The fairy landed deftly on a nearby tree stump, folded her wings behind her back, straightened her dress, and used a dew drop hanging from a nearby flower to look at her reflection, smiling to herself with approval then turned and calmly replied,

"I'm Mabel," then the little person, looking at the sweet treat in Dottie's hand said with urgency, "well come on, come on, I'm famished, can't wait around all day, you know."

"Oh, ok, you can have a little then, here you go Mabel." She took the smallest piece of sugared bread and passed it carefully down to entirely fill her tiny, outstretched hands. "By the way, I do like your dress and your shoes, they're really beautiful, I'd love to wear something like them, instead of all the second-

hand ones my sister Viola doesn't like or has grown out of."
With an aerial curtsy of thanks, Mabel took a bite of the bread,
and she flew down to sit back on the mossy rock.

"Thanks, so what's your own name then?" Mabel asked nonchalantly, happily munching away on the sugary treat. Dottie,
beginning to come out of her initial shock at this magical sight
replied,

"Oh, ahem, my name is Dottie Moorehead, nice to meet you
Mabel. Do you live in these woods?" Dottie asked hopefully.

"No, but we come here every summer. I've noticed you in the
woods before and how kindly you interact with the other creatures that share the land with you; you're different from most
tall-walkers. We don't usually allow you folks to see us, not unless we are sure you have a kind heart. What's all this about
your sister getting all the nice clothes then? She gets all the best
stuff, and you get nothing?" asked Mabel.

"Well," said Dottie, "it's like this...." Dottie went on to describe
to Mabel how Viola was the older sister and so her mother
would buy her new clothes but how Dottie only ever got the
ones Viola had grown too big for or had just rejected out of
hand. This was not as bad for Dottie as it seemed however, and
she explained to Mabel that many of the dresses Viola rejected
were the very style and pattern that Dottie would have chosen
to wear anyway. Mabel listened intently and nodded and made
noises to indicate she knew exactly what Dottie was talking
about. Dottie explained how she always managed to wear her
favourite articles of clothing although somewhat larger than
her own size but felt frustrated about how big they were. She
mimed for Mabel how her mother would say, "You'll grow into
them in time, Dottie, and you're growing at such a rate now
that there would be no reason to get your size as you'll have
grown out of them in no time at all." It did not help much and
left Dottie feeling a bit second best. She felt comfortable explaining and complaining to her new little friend. Dottie told

how she loved dresses with flower patterns on them whereas Viola on the other hand preferred plain colours and the plainer the better. How she was mean to Dottie for no reason at all and how she was always picking her nose, which was an awfully bad habit to get into. Mabel sat there and listened and smiled, taking it all in. Then when Dottie had got it all out and had run out of steam Mabel just said,

"You think you have it bad? I have a *brother*. Sisters are one thing, but brothers are the worst." The two friends looked at one another for a moment then both burst out in laughter. Their giggles and chuckles echoed around the forest and even the trees seemed to join in their gaiety. Eventually, Mabel asked, "so, you'll meet me again? I'd love to stay longer but I have no time just now, in an awful rush you see, perhaps we can meet here again the day after tomorrow when I'm not in such a great hurry, I might bring some of my friends and maybe even my brother? "

"Yes, yes, please let's," Dottie replied excitedly. Then after she had eaten all the bread and sugar, taking extra care to savour every morsel, she fluttered around Dottie's head,

"It was so lovely to meet you Dottie, and by the way, I like your dress too, especially as it has all those flowers on it, I do love flowers," she said with a smile. Mabel did a few loop the loops in the air and thanked Dottie for sharing her sugary bread and butter sandwiches, brushed her tiny hands together to dislodge any grains of sugar, and then, with that she was gone. The birds were singing joyfully in the trees and Dottie wondered for a moment if she had imagined the whole thing. But then smiled, knowing her life would never be quite the same from then on. This pleased her greatly and she giggled to herself as she finished up the remainder of her little feast. She was excited but quite unfazed by her meeting with Mabel the fairy and wanted to know more about her and her magical world. She really hoped Mabel would be true to her word and come visit again. Instinctively, she knew it was best to keep her meeting with Mabel to herself for now. Dottie felt Viola's derision many times before when she had tried to tell her even the most mundane of discoveries. She decided to wait for Mabel's next visit even if only to prove to herself it had all really happened; she hoped it had.

CHAPTER 8

Sweet Tooth

Her mother and grandmother's parsimoniousness was the bane of Dottie's sweet tooth. Dottie never understood the meaning of rationing and so, obtaining sugar, and other sweet things, from her grandmother's larder was her only source of a tempting treat. However, while her mother did not believe in spoiling her daughters, she would, on occasion, bring her children to the sweet shop in the village. Coincidentally, the day after Dottie had first met Mabel, her mother was home and decided to visit the local village on a rare shopping trip. Dottie's mother brought herself and Viola to the confectioners where they could feast their eyes on all the colourful delights. There was shelf-upon-shelf of hardboiled sweets and jellies of all shapes and colours, going right up to the ceiling. To Dottie each visit was a pure joy for the senses.

"Well, what would you like, Dottie?" asked their mother.

"I'll have a little of everything please Mummy," she said, thinking she would share her treats with her new fairy friend, Mabel, so she could enjoy something more than her sugary bread.

"You can only have a few of your favourites dear, and the same goes for your sister, you know you must look after your teeth too my dears."

"Yes, Dottie, don't be such a greedy guts, your stupid teeth will all rot in your head, and they'll all fall out of your mouth, one by one and you won't be able to eat any more sweets ever again, not ever," said her sister looking over at her and

25

smirking with the knowledge that Dottie wouldn't be getting what she wanted.

"Now, now, Viola, there's no need to be so mean to your little sister," their mother scolded. Dottie felt shocked by the image of her teeth falling out and wondered how to avoid this, and also, she didn't want to harm her new friend with such horrors, but still, somehow, she managed to eat some of her own sweets, even after this dire warning. She felt she could not explain to her mother or sister that it was not greediness that made her ask, but instead she was trying to get a little of each type of treat for Mabel to sample. She knew how much she would delight in the colourful and tasty confections, but she also knew if she confided in her family about her new magical friend then Viola would just mock her and call her names. So, Dottie kept her counsel about Mabel, thinking it better to be seen as a little greedy rather than taken for a liar.

This quest for tasty treats was where Dottie's interest in natural plants first started. When her grandmother showed her the many edible sweet berries and wild plants dotted around the hedgerows surrounding the farm, Dottie was hooked. Her grandmother's knowledge on foraging was extensive, as it was for many of her generation. She instructed Dottie on which fruits or plants were safe to eat. She warned her inquisitive little granddaughter of other plants that were not edible at all, and indeed, some were highly poisonous, while others tasted awfully bitter altogether.

"Now, Dottie, you can suck the juice from the stem of this flower, it might stop you stealing the sugar from my cupboards," her grandmother said, fixing her granddaughter with a scowl, while she picked up the wildflowers from outside the back-kitchen door. Her grandmother gave a small 'harumph' of satisfaction at having shown her granddaughter that she was wise to her tricks and was, to put it in her own words, "no fool at all!" Dottie would suck the juice from the stems of these floral edible treats, just as her grandmother showed her, discovering the delicious rewards inside. This knowledge suddenly opened up a whole new world to the sweet-deprived little girl; it was the one and only gift she had ever received from her grandmother and one for which she was eternally grateful. When they were pruning the blackcurrant bushes in the autumn near the apple trees, Dottie would take all the pruned twigs and stick them in and around all the hedgerows surrounding the farmland, she was a very enterprising and sagacious young lady as she was imagining the bounty that lay ahead the following year at berry harvesting time.

September was one of her favourite months because this was when the blackberries were ripe on the brambles. She would spend all afternoon picking out the best ones, gathering more than she could ever eat herself, for her feast back in the kitchen. There, she would sprinkle a little sugar over them and spoon them into her mouth until she could not eat anymore. The next morning, Dottie was up bright and early. She had returned home with a large punnet of blackberries and set it down on the kitchen table to share them with Viola. As she was eating her berries, she forgot herself and her earlier plan in keeping her own council by casually mentioning to her sister that she had met a fairy yesterday. Viola was incensed,

"Stop making things up Dottie, there's no such thing as fairies, they're just for little children, stupid little babies, that is what you are, you're a stupid little baby," Viola snapped with venom in her voice.

"But…but…. I really did see her, I really did!" said Dottie. "Why won't you ever believe me? Her name's Mabel, she was so tiny and so pretty…. I swear. It's true. It's TRUE!!!" Dottie entreated. Viola's eyes narrowed,

"Oh, don't be so ridiculous, you're always going to be a liar. You have to make up having imaginary friends because no one wants to be your real friend anyway."

"I don't know why I ever bother telling you ANYTHING," said a tearful Dottie, feeling hurt. Next thing, Viola slammed her plate down on the kitchen table, rolled her eyes upwards and sighed with exasperation, stood up and stormed out of the kitchen. Besides feeling hurt at her sister's unjustified attack, what was more surprising to the sweet-toothed Dottie, was not the vicious attack Viola inflicted on her, but, that her sister was not even interested in sharing her delicious collection of freshly picked berries. Dottie had a tear rolling down her little face, around her lips was tainted with purple berry juice and she was wide-eyed, more in confusion than shock, as to how Viola was able to resist such a sweet treat – Dottie never could. She looked up from the table as her grandmother entered the room to ask what all the commotion was about; Dottie quickly wiped away a tear, just shrugged her shoulders and continued finishing her berries.

"You would want to hurry up and get in the last of those berries before the first frost comes, *The Fairy Blast* they call it. They'll be no good to eat after that." Dottie was shocked with this news.

"Really Gran? Are you sure?" Smugly nodding her head with her eyes closed, her grandmother assured her that this was so. Immediately, Dottie picked up her plethora of metal buckets and wicker punnets as if her life depended on it and went straight back out to collect even more of those sweet juicy berries. She could get lost in the simple act of picking those ripe, jewel-like berries. Once she started, she would find it hard to stop, and she soon forgot all about her sister's meanness, while always finding just one more delicious fruit dangling from a bramble, tempting her to just pick them all away till the sun started to go down. How she loved what she began to call "the berry madness," her little fingers so stained with berry juice they would eventually become numb from the acids in the fruits, but this did not deter Dottie and she clambered over the hedgerows, her pots, and punnets full to the brim with those luscious, glistening blackberries.

CHAPTER 9

Nell and the Berry Madness

It was when out on this last berry-picking mission of the season that Dottie met her neighbour Nell, while she too was out foraging in nature's bounty. Nell lived in one of the cottages on the borders of the farm; these were historically rented out for a peppercorn rent by Dottie's father. Dottie's grandmother referred to Nell as one of the 'cottage people,' and said that they were good people who would always help you out with anything. No one knew exactly how old Nell was, evidently, she was in her twilight years, but she looked very fit and strong, and walked with the steadiness and vigour of a woman in her prime. The clothes she wore looked like something from another era but always suited her and seemed to lend her an air of timelessness and wisdom. Nell always had great time for little Dottie as a year earlier Dottie was in a bit of a predicament in that she had gotten herself stuck up a tree and was unable to get down. Nell had been out mushroom picking and happened to be passing by at that moment. Much to an adventurer like Dottie's embarrassment, she had to admit that she was in a spot of bother.

"Hello Nell…. Hello there…please…. I'm stuck, I can't get down from here," Dottie shouted.

"Oh, dearie me Dottie, how did you ever manage to get up there in the first place?" Nell asked in amusement looking up at the little girl high in the branches of an ancient oak tree.

"Oh, I wanted to see how high I could climb to get a better view around the countryside, and I just went up a bit too high." "Don't worry child," said Nell reassuringly, "I happen to have a ladder here so just grab hold of it and climb down slowly." Dottie heeded the old lady's advice and gingerly made her way down the wooden ladder.

"That's it, well done, one step at a time, that's it," Nell instructed. As Dottie nodded, and did as she was told, she felt comforted by Nell's calming voice.

"Thank you, thank you very much. I really don't know what I'd have done if you hadn't come along, I'd probably have been stuck up there for ever!" Nell laughed at Dottie's dramatics, "I pass by here all the time, so I think you would have been rescued eventually." As Dottie walked away from the oak tree, she could not help wondering how did that ladder appear, or was it somewhere out of sight all the time? But now she noticed that the ladder seemed to have vanished once more and was nowhere to be seen. Dottie was a little taken aback by the mystery of the ladder but as they got talking, she soon forgot all about her earlier trauma. To Dottie, Nell was a kind and friendly neighbour and, more importantly, interested in the same things Dottie was interested in during the autumn months; the wild berries, and that was good enough for Dottie.

"This is a great spot for the sweetest berries I got punnet loads this morning," Nell said; as she pointed towards a thicket with lots of blackberries hanging like baubles on a Christmas tree. "They weren't ripe enough yesterday, but it seems that today they are all perfect." Dottie, also a connoisseur of the bramble fruit, was impressed by Nell's local knowledge and expertise. Nell continued, "I've been picking them myself the last few days just over there by the fairy fort. I love them for jam-making, and have so many jars, too many in fact, would you like some to take back to your mother? Dottie squealed with delight,

"Oh, that would be great, we all love blackberry jam, Mummy will be so pleased, thank you." Dottie did her best to remember her manners and be polite to Nell. Dottie respected her; she was so different to her grandmother, always so relaxed and spoke to Dottie as a kindred spirit.

"My pleasure, I make so much of the stuff, and I'll never manage to eat it all myself, once I start making jam, I find I always seem make too much. I'll make you up a basket to back to the farm." Dottie was delighted with Nell's generosity and was already thinking of how she was going to smother the jam all over her soda bread and butter later for tea, delicious. Nell, noting the delight on little Dottie's face, chuckled to herself.

"Time to finish up now dearie, the sun is nearly set, let's go back to my cottage, wash our hands and I'll get that basket packed for you. I'll even help you carry it back to your house." Later, as they walked the pathway back to the farmhouse, Nell commented nonchalantly on wondering if the fairies would be around for much longer this year as it looked like there might be a frost that night. Dottie was astonished at Nell's candour,

"Nell, do you believe in fairies too?" she gasped.

"Believe in them?" replied Nell. "You may as well ask if I believe in these blackberries. Fairies are as real as you and I, in fact, I was only with them in the woods last week," Nell said smiling at the little girl.

"Oh, thank goodness; I wasn't sure if I'd just dreamed it all up, but I saw one too, yesterday. My sister thinks I'm lying Nell, but I really met one; her name was Mabel," she said, relieved to be able to share her discovery.

"Oh, I know Mabel very well, that one's always in a hurry, that's half her trouble, once she gets some sugar into that tiny tummy of hers, she's as buzzy as a bumblebee in spring. You mustn't mind what your sister says, my dear, you know what you saw, so trust in yourself, believe in what you see,"

Nell replied with a knowing smile. "Some people cannot see the magic that is all around them, so they believe in nothing." "I'm meeting Mabel again tomorrow," said Dottie, smiling. "Oh, that will be nice dear, say hello from me, won't you? They usually leave when the first frost falls; then they all head home. They won't return until the beginning of next summer. I might pop by myself before they leave to wish them farewell, just to be mannerly," Nell said. "Mabel doesn't show herself to just anybody you know, she's very discerning, so you should be really honoured that she chose to reveal herself to you, and not to your sister, Dottie my dear."

Mabel and the Fairies

The very next morning before breakfast Dottie was out of her bed in a flash. She ran to the window to look out over the front lawn and in the direction of the woods. The early morning sun was shining down, and a light mist hung over the meadow. She could see in the shade there was the lightest touch of frost on the grass, so she knew then she had to hurry. Dottie quickly got dressed and rushed downstairs for her breakfast.

"What are you doing? I suppose you think you are going to meet your fairy friends again Dottie," sneered Viola. Both sisters locked eyes and then Viola shouted; "GRAN! GRAN! Dottie is taking more sugar from the cupboard behind your back, look, she's sprinkling it all over her bread and butter. She said she's taking it to the fairies Gran, Dottie is so stupid she believes in fairies, GRAN! GRAN!!" Viola was now shouting it out louder and louder trying her best to get her sister into as much trouble as she could, as she had always done. "Dottie is doing something bold behind your back Gran." Viola was forever trying to get Dottie into trouble with her grandmother. As she was preparing some more tasty treats in readiness for her meeting with Mabel, Dottie glared angrily at Viola. Whilst doing so, she was also keeping one eye on her grandmother to avoid being caught in the act. Viola was doing her level best to thwart Dottie's plans and was leaning as far back on her chair as she could, their Grandmother was in the pantry and a little out of earshot, so Viola tried to lean further back still. Suddenly, the legs of her chair slid, and she came crashing down with a hard bang, landing in a heap on the floor. Viola started to cry with the shock and her Grandmother rushed in as fast as she could to see what all the commotion was about.

"Viola, are you alright love? What in goodness' name is going on in here? Just what have you done to your sister you bad girl?" she demanded, looking over at Dottie.

"Why are you looking at me? I didn't do anything!" Dottie remarked with her eyes wide open. Viola was more shook than hurt. She was trying as she might to explain that it was all Dottie's fault. She was crying, but as she had been winded by the fall onto the terracotta tiled floor, she couldn't get the words out at all.

"You could have broken your neck; you should never lean back on any chair like that," their grandmother said, tut-tutting away to herself. "Are you sure you had nothing to do with this Dottie?" her Grandmother quizzed, her eyes narrowing further. Dottie was annoyed that her grandmother was blaming her.

"How could I have done anything? I'm MILES away from her" she protested.

"Don't get cheeky with me, young lady," her grandmother snapped. Once she knew her sister was okay and nothing was broken, and being conscious of the time, Dottie raced out the door, bread and sweets wrapped and hidden in her pocket. She ran up to the woods as fast as her little legs could carry her, leaving Viola to try and explain how Dottie could have had anything to do with her kitchen trauma. Somehow, no matter what, Dottie would always be blamed in some way, but right now she did not care, all she could think of was getting to meet with Mabel again.

As soon as she got to the woods, she was looking around everywhere for her fairy friend. She sat on an old fallen tree trunk, she was swinging her legs on it for what seemed like an eternity while a robin landed on a higher branch to keep her company. She called out Mabel's name a few times,

"Mabel, Maa-belll… are you there?" She heard her name being called and suddenly there was Mabel, but she wasn't on her own this time, some of her fellow fairy friends were with her and Dottie was so excited to be introduced to them. One-by-one they all introduced themselves by name, took a bow, and then fluttered around her head; their little wings buzzing and causing Dottie's hair to flick and flutter as they whizzed close by.

"Hello Mabel," Dottie said excitedly. "Hello everybody!" Noticing the expectant look on their magical little faces, Dottie proclaimed, "Don't worry, I didn't forget," producing the wrapped parcels of sweets and sugary bread from her pocket, "It was awfully hard to resist scoffing the lot though," Dottie confessed. "I didn't think you were coming but I even kept some blackberry jam on a slice for you all too," she said proudly. Following a momentary pause from their rapt attention to the delights of the colourful confections, the fairies broke out into spontaneous applause and cheering,

"Oh, great stuff, thanks, we'll enjoy that," Mabel said, assembling all her little friends together to receive their treats. Dottie thought it was lucky they were all so small as she had more than enough of the treats and buttery, sugary and jammy bread to go round, while still having enough for herself.

"Have you been waiting long for us Dottie?" asked Dorm, a yellow-coloured little fellow with shiny pink wings. He had bright red hair with some miniature ivy leaves bound around his head, set at a jaunty angle. He was wearing tiny golden boots and had a sparkly glow about him.

"Well yes, Dorm, I was waiting all morning long," she said, sounding a little bit annoyed. Her annoyance was not with the fairies but only from the effort it took to resist eating her treats until they arrived. "A little robin friend was keeping me company though, and I was just happy to get away from my sister, she's always being horrible to me and always trying to get me into trouble with my granny."

"Oh, that's just terrible Dottie – but I do know what you mean," said Dorm sympathetically. "Sisters can be like that, my own sister is forever taking my stuff and making me grumpy." Just then, Mabel whizzed by and snatched some of Dorm's bread and jam, ate it with delight saying,

"Thank you, brother dearest." Dorm looked at his, now much diminished, piece of bread and jam and, with a resigned sign, and slump of his little shoulders, he ate the remnants of his treat and then looked to Dottie.

"See what I mean?!" Dottie nodded in solidarity with him and felt a lot better now she had shared her thoughts.

"Were you all somewhere nice this morning?" Dottie asked.

"We were taking in the last of the sunshine before we start our journey back home," Dorm announced.

"I'm so sad you are going. Why did I not meet you all before now? I wish I had; we could have had such fun all summer long," said a rather forlorn Dottie.

"Well, even if you couldn't see us before, we were always nearby. We're all very intrigued by your antics, and sometimes, have stepped in to avoid you doing yourself a mischief. But mostly, we spend our days here enjoying the sunshine; we must store up its energy so when we go home, we can carry a little of that warmth and energy inside. That is why we come here every summer you see, it's quite unique here, and we love the multicoloured light in your realm. In our home, the light is of a singular waveband, we have none of the wonderful colours you have here. Your sunlight makes us transparent so it's very hard to spot us." There was general agreement from Mabel and the rest of her friends on hearing Dorm's explanation. Dottie's face brightened and she said,

"I could tell someone was around me, but I just thought I was imagining it all, so that was all of you?"

"No, it was your imagination!" she heard one wisecracking fairy reply. She could hear slightly nervous giggles at the bemused look on her face, but then, she burst into laughter and everyone else joined in too. Fairies love to laugh and so did Dottie. As the sun began to sink lower in the sky, Mabel flew up and hovered in front of Dottie, then she sang the most beautiful song, in the most beautiful voice, that Dottie had ever heard. The song told the story of the fairies' far-off land and how wonderful it was there, all the others broke into beautiful harmonies and enjoyed the melody of this song of their homeland, 'Florestael.' But their ability to adjust their songs to suit any occasion saw them mention their journey to Dottie's land to play and enjoy the sunshine. Dorm then performed a solo where he recounted, in song, humorously of course, some of little Dottie's antics. This delighted her and she clapped along in time with the melody. The chorus of fairies raised their voices louder and louder then suddenly, they stopped as both Mabel and Dorm duetted in a big finale, one trying to outdo the other; they were quite the attention-seekers. Each, in turn, tried to hit an increasingly higher note, Mabel hit a B, then Dorm aimed for an octave above, but failed, miserably. All that came out was a tortured squeak. Dorm looked so embarrassed. Mabel stood stock still....her eyes wide and staring at her brother, unsure of how to react. Dorm turned to the assembled chorus, and to Dottie, shrugged his shoulders and said, "I squeaked!"

"What did he say?" asked some of the fairies.

" …'believe the fellow said that he SQUEAKED!" answered some others.

"Oh yes, he most definitely squeaked!!" came a reply from another fairy.

After a long pause, spontaneously, they all burst into rapturous applause, all heartily cheered and praised Dorm for giving it his best attempt. Dorm's smile grew wide, and Mabel patted his back and said,
"Well done brother, you're the best squeaker I know."
Then everyone broke down into joyous laughter again and sang once more with gusto:

As the fairy frost descends
Telling us fairies it's time to depart.
To our lovely land of Florestael
The land so close to each one's heart
The clock tick tocks and signals all
To gather now and play their part.
Fly now, fly quick to Florestael!
Beware that fairy frost my friends.

This frost can harm a fairy's wing,
and turn them all tattered and torn,
this fairy frost you see is no good thing,
it can leave us so forlorn.

So off we go to Florestael,
the land where the fairies dwell,
Florestael, Florestael,
Never gets frosty in Florestael.
The land where the fairies dwell.

It's time to say goodbye,
but there's no need to shed a tear.
As we'll be flying high.
Back here again next year.
Now the autumn leaves begin to fall,
crunch and turn brown in the hall,

'cause fairies' wings and frost,
you see, do not mix well, at all.

So off we go to Florestael,
the land where the fairies dwell,
Florestael, Florestael,
Never gets frosty in Florestael.
The land where the fairies dwell.

It has such a glow so bright,
we never get sad and low, on occasion,
where we all sing of the fight.
Back in the days of the great invasion
stories of our ancestors dwell,
of Ethel and Pul, who heroically fell,
fighting to protect the future for us all,
where we triumphed and felt so tall.

So off we go to Florestael,
the land where the fairies dwell,
Florestael, Florestael,
Never gets frosty in Florestael.
The land where the fairies dwell.

We head off to Blusfloct,
With flowers to smell,
which the frost does quell
All travel there to dock.
for the summer spell
we can watch little Dottie play,
meet the great Nell and stay,
to sing and party all day.

So off we go to Florestael,

the land where the fairies dwell,
Florestael, Florestael,
Never gets frosty in Florestael.
The land where the fairies dwell.

The light in Florestael,
So bright it sounds like a bell.
We-all-dwell-in-Flor-est-ael.

Dottie clapped and cheered when they reached their big finale, and laughed with delight at being mentioned in their song, "Bravo! Bravo! Encore!! Now why can't I sing like that?" Dottie asked jocosely. They took their bows and fell about laughing. Dottie had so many more questions to ask them about 'Florestael,' and most especially, if one day she would be able to visit them?

"You can visit us anytime you choose to, Dottie, but first you will have to learn all about us, and Nell will help you there, you can ask her anything, she is such a lovely being, all the fairies love her," said Mabel. Sensing Dottie was a little sad about the fairies impending departure, Mabel clapped her hands excitedly and said, "Come on now, Dottie, let's join in the festivities." They all danced, sang, and did play-flights in the woods and soon Dottie was lost in all the fun. A little later Nell arrived, all greeted her warmly, and she them, they had been waiting for her to bid her farewell,

"Hello, Mabel dear, how have you been since last week?" Nell enquired. Mabel nodded with a smile indicating that all was well, but then a more serious look came across Nell's face as she asked, "Did you sort that important matter we discussed?" Mabel's continence seemed to lose its levity as she replied, "Yes, all sorted now till next year, I hope." The two seemed to engage in a nonverbal communication that seemed to last a few minutes then once again the bright smiles returned to their faces, and they re-joined the celebrations. "Nell, you must bring Dottie to visit us sometime," she suggested.

"Oh, I will indeed, that is if she would like to come of course?"

"Yes please!!" said Dottie excitedly, a little worse for wear after all the sugary treats. "I'd love to go." Mabel smiled at Nell and Dottie, the little fairy's face now seeming wise, and her voice taking on a regal tone. "There will always be a welcome for you among the fairy folk," she proclaimed. As the sun began to set on that last truly warm evening before the turn of the year, when late summer becomes early Autumn, the fairies began their journey back to their homeland. Nell and Dottie could hear their songs fading gradually, they merrily flitted through the evening air, and then they were gone. Dottie felt sad at their departure. Nell, sensing the little girl's sadness, put a comforting hand on her shoulder saying,

"don't worry we will visit them in the wintertime. Now, let's go back to my cottage and I will make us a lovely cup of cocoa before you head back up home.

"With a marshmallow?" asked Dottie, still frazzled from all that sugar,

"I think you have had enough," chuckled Nell.

"I think you might be right!" Dottie agreed as they walked back to Nell's cottage.

Jupiter

As the days shortened and autumn began to draw in, Dottie longed for that trip to Florestael when she would travel with Nell to see Mabel and the other fairy folk again. The weeks passed, the leaves turned, and the sun sank a little lower each day.

Every time Dottie would ask, "When?" Nell would try to reassure the impatient little girl by saying, "Soon enough!"

But to a child even a day can seem like an eternity, so eventually Dottie had given up on that day ever arriving. Initially, to distract herself, Dottie started to focus on inventing new games to play and busied herself with being outside in the garden. She spent her time playing in the fallen leaves and looking at all the different little bugs and creatures, pondering how they too prepared for the winter. School also formed part of her daily routine which she grudgingly accepted as something she must do, but once Dottie had returned home from her morning classes she would sprint from the car, run across the fields and traipse around the farmland for the rest of the day.

She loved to explore her kingdom, but being an adventurer, she generally got herself into all sorts of mischief. On several occasions, despite having been warned by her father of the dangers, she managed to get into the field where the big bull, Jupiter, was kept, and for some unknown reason, this bull had taken a huge dislike to her.

After another of her father's trips abroad, he recounted to her his first visit to a bull ring in Spain, telling tales of the daring matador holding up his crimson cape and challenging the noble bull to mortal combat. The furious beast charging, head down, "TORO! TORO!" the spectators would shout, the bull narrowly missing the matador as he deftly stepped aside, the crowd would gasp, "OLÉ!" All would applaud the matador's skill and shower him with red roses. The excitement of the daring-do really appealed to Dottie. She just had to try it out for herself and face down that grumpy old bull on the farm.

One sunny Saturday morning in November, she took her grandmother's Christmas-red tablecloth out of the press. She donned a little waistcoat which she had decorated by pinning dried flowers and roses on it. Finally, she found one of her grandmother's wide-brimmed hats from the top of the wardrobe, which took quite a bit of mountaineering finesse to claim, and then skipped out the door and up to the top field. Once there, she put on the waistcoat, her hat was set at a jaunty angle, and she unfurled the red tablecloth. She saw Jupiter on the crest of the field and started to try and get his attention. Her plan was that one day, after a lot of practice, she would be skilled enough to stand in that same Spanish arena that her father had told her about. She would gain acclaim for fearlessly facing down those great black bulls. Her fame would spread, and at every tournament the spectators would applaud wildly and cheer on her exploits. He had shown her posters from Spain depicting legendary bullfighters in their colourful regalia. The painted images showed the matador mid-action and always in a most dynamic pose. Dottie would imagine the scene, "OLÉ! OLÉ!" they would shout "Olé Senorita Dottie!" She started to shout at Jupiter in the top field,

"TORO! TORO! Come here Jupiter." She stood up straight, back arched, and tablecloth held out to her side. Dottie used a broomstick underneath the cloth to keep it spread wide, while waving and flicking it till, trying to catch the bull's attention...and it did. As he began to scrape the earth with his front hoof, she could see the enraged creature snort powerfully down his nostrils. He noticed her alright, and he did not like this little pest in HIS field one little bit. He began to charge. Dottie thought he would try and put his head through the red cloth, that all his attention would be drawn to it, but it wasn't. The red tablecloth was of no interest at all, and his main target was Dottie. She thought better of it and quickly dived back over the fence and out of harm's way, leaving Jupiter goring her grandmother's tablecloth to shreds and grinding it into the dirt with his powerful hooves.

She did not give up though, she found another red tablecloth to use and thought Jupiter only needed a bit of training to get the hang of it. With some coaxing he would learn what to do. But Jupiter had a mind of his own, and each time Dottie entered his field, he seemed angrier than the last. He had not the slightest bit of interest in those red tablecloths. Instead, he would charge straight for her, the ground would shake under his immense weight, and she just managed to get out of his way in the nick of time. Each occasion ended with him ripping apart yet another tablecloth, scraping the dirt, and creating a massive dust cloud under his furious hooves. From then on, the moment Jupiter saw Dottie, he would come charging straight for her, she had many lucky escapes from him.

But on one fateful occasion, her wellies got stuck in the heavy mud at the bottom of the field. There had been heavy rain the night before, she was stuck fast as the outraged bull barrelled toward her at full speed, this time there was no escape. Dottie was frozen to the spot. Then, suddenly, she felt a pair of strong hands grab her, haul her out of her wellington boots, and safely out of harm's way. It was her father, who happened to be there on this occasion. He saw what was unfolding and ran straight in to rescue her before Jupiter could reach her. He was ashen faced,

"You can never trust a bull Dottie," he chided. "Do you hear me? You must NEVER tease Jupiter and never, ever, turn your back on him. Do you understand?"

"But Daddy, I was only trying to be like one of those matadors," Dottie explained, tears now welling-up; feeling like she had done something awfully wrong to have displeased her father so. Her father didn't know whether to be angry or just to hug her as they had BOTH got such a fright.

On another occasion, Jupiter kept her held hostage for an entire day in the yard, before her parents arrived home to find Dottie on the top bar of the crush, hanging on uncomfortably with a sheepish grin on her face, while he was bellowing and snorting violently while scraping the ground below her. This horrified her parents and they felt she was out of control; something had to be done, as she had no one around to keep an eye on her. They asked Nell if she would be the child's guardian while they were away on research trips abroad. Nell was more than happy to take the young child under her wing. And so, it was arranged that Dottie would call over in the mornings to wherever Nell would be. Many mornings Dottie would find Nell in the Moorehead's walled garden tending to her herbs and plants and generally trying to boss the old gardener, Molloy around. Molloy took her administrations with good humour and would often refer to Nell as "The Sergeant Major," but never to her face of course, he had served his country with honour and was a brave man, but he was not foolhardy. Dottie gravitated towards him during her time in the garden. They had built up a good working relationship and she became his occasional assistant around the garden; they often walked around the path checking when the loganberries were ripe or inspecting the apple trees to see when they needed a pruning. Molloy had endless patience and enjoyed answering

Dottie's horticultural questions; they would be seen conversing about the right way to cultivate the various plants and best practices for keeping carrot fly at bay. Around the farmhouse front lawn, he took the time to answer Dottie whenever she asked about the many species of tall trees and plants around the country house and in the walled garden.

Previously, the grounds had been tended by up to eight gardeners, but now, it was all down to Molloy. These days people rarely asked him about his extensive knowledge of the gardens and wider landscape, or of the names of local areas and townlands, he had missed that. So now, with the inquisitive Dottie seeing it all anew, it had enlivened the old man and he delighted in sharing as much of his vast knowledge with her as possible. He also coached her in the craft of beekeeping; a craft handed down to him by his father and his father before him. Molloy had weaved skeps which he would have Dottie hold underneath the big Elderberry tree during swarming season and have her catch the swarm that he would shake from its branches. Dottie marvelled when Molloy would spread a white sheet on the ground under the skep full of bees and then watch for hours as the bees marched their way up that sheet and into the clean WBC hive Molloy had prepared.

"Let the bees do the work Dottie, no need to rush them, they know where they want to go, and once the queen goes in the rest of her handmaidens will follow...just watch and see." Sure enough, soon Molloy would point to the entrance of the hive and declare, "She's In!" Dottie wondered how he could be certain, so Molloy pointed to the little line of bees fanning their wings at the entrance, "See Dottie, they are fanning to guide the rest of their sisters in, that's how you know the queen is already installed." Dottie would help him weed the vegetable patch, this would tire her out and stop her getting up to any more mischief. Her job was to weed around the carrot drills and, although she was a reluctant appointee to this task at first, she soon got so caught up in making sure that the carrots were totally weed-free that she would get lost in her work. She would stand back admiring those pristinely weeded rows and compare them to the unruly ones. Dottie would be absorbed in the act of weeding; attending carefully around each carrot and making sure that every one of them was perfect. She would gather all the wilted weeds into a small toy wheelbarrow Molloy had found for her. Dottie would load the weeds, one handful after another, and once piled high, she would wheel it unsteadily to the compost heap. Wheelbarrows, despite their ubiquity, are far more unwieldy that one might think. It took Dottie some time to get used to wheelbarrow driving, and she found it a bit of a handful to operate. But she was nothing if not determined, so with her tongue stuck out the side of her mouth she would wheel load after load, along the gravel pathway and over to the big compost heap near the giant rhubarb patch. Depending on the weather and temperature, sometimes steam would rise from the heap. Dottie would trek back to the garden and, under the leaf canopy with that steamy mist rising, she would imagine she was in an Amazonian jungle. Wearing the pith helmet Molloy gave her for her veil when she was beekeeping, she looked very much like a little explorer as she moved slowly through the tenebrous thicket of giant plants and shrubs. This work would keep her busy for most of her mornings and Nell could see how eager Dottie was to learn about nature.

For all Molloy's knowledge on the gardens, it was Nell who taught Dottie more of the medicinal qualities of many of the plants Molloy might simple have called "auld weeds." Nell and Dottie perused through the woods on some of the land and every morning would open the green wooden door to the outer walled garden and went through. It felt otherworldly in that garden; with Molloy tending to some rhubarb or spreading horse manure around his prized rose bushes. Dottie's nose would wrinkle at the smell, she'd pinch her nose and try to block it out. This made the old gardener laugh and declare, "Fine healthy smell, we should have a great display this year!"

"Will the rhubarb be ready for harvest before Michaelmas?" enquired Nell.

"Indeed'in it will be Nell, indeed'in it will," he replied then returned to his odorous work.

A little later at the potting shed Nell beckoned to her young charge.

"Now Dottie, I have been growing some wonderful herbs and you can help me to transplant them out of their little seed trays and into their own pots. We will be placing them into one of the greenhouses. The warmth will encourage them to grow strong and plentiful before we transplant out into the herb garden in a month or so." In the inner garden, Nell let an entire area grow wild; nettles, burdock, borage, and foxgloves along with poppies, and other wildflowers flourished. There was a constant buzzing of life among the foliage. Nothing was grown for its beauty alone but also for its usefulness. Dottie's parents never came into that inner garden, quite frankly, they would have been horrified if they saw all the weeds growing there. Nell was the only one that did venture in there; it was her space to contemplate and to learn about the many uses of those wonderful plants. "Remember Dottie, an awful lot of these plants are poisonous to those who don't know anything about them, so you must be very, very, careful until I show you how to treat each one. Once you have this knowledge then you can use the plants to get the best out of them. Never think you can pick or chew or eat any plant unless you have been shown exactly which are safe to eat or use and which are not. Some are most deadly dangerous, even the prettiest looking ones, so always be wary and wait for expert advice." She picked some interesting looking plant up in her hands and rubbed it between her fingers to inhale its great aroma, there was rose-hips breeching through the nettles along with so many other rare and wonderful species that Nell had cultivated over decades. Dottie found the herbs very interesting indeed as not all could be used in the kitchen. "Now Dottie, some of these are for my potions and this will be your introduction to following in my footsteps as a herbologist. You must attend to your own scholastic duties and gain an understanding of the practical sciences and the arts of course, but here, in my part of the garden, this is where you shall gain the wisdom of the ages, taught to us by the elders and known only to those with a pure heart and an open mind. This will be your bucolic university where you will learn the sorcerer's craft. Most importantly, we shall have fun here Dottie, would you like that?"

"That would be great Nell, I would love to know more."

Dottie treasured that old potting shed, she noted, on entering, one could detect a sweet, fresh earthy smell, not musty, just dried and compacted from centuries of footfall which had burnished the reddy-brown clay beneath their feet and, over the years, evolved into a beautiful shiny surface. Dottie had a naturally inquisitive mind and a boundless thirst for knowledge, which the elderly lady recognised as many of the same qualities she herself had possessed as a child. Dottie would bring some new weed that she did not recognise and ask Nell to identify it for her. Nell would examine the plant with her well-worn loupe and tell Dottie the plant's native name, its name in Latin, and detail any qualities the plant might have. That same curiosity, and nascent ability Nell had once displayed in her own youth, was now shining through Dottie and the wise old lady could plainly see that this little girl showed real promise. With all this, Dottie's time was fully taken up and her days of being a tearaway matador faded into distant memory, except for Jupiter that is – he never forgot.

The Apprenticeship Begins

U nbeknownst to Dottie, that day Nell rescued her from being stuck up a tree was no chance encounter. Nell always had one eye out for Dottie while she was in the woods gathering herbs and wild plants for her potions and cures. The fact Dottie's parents had engaged Nell's services as a guardian was fortuitous. Over the weeks and days as they gardened and chatted, Dottie would ask Nell about all the wild plants and herbs that grew in and around the hedgerows and on the boarders of the farmland,

"I have something to show you just here, now you must get down close to the ground and have a good look at this flower growing in the grass there. No need to pick it, as that will only disturb it from its growing. This plant, and its flower, give the earth great feedback to help regulate the weather systems; so, we do not have too much wet weather in winter, nor too much dry weather in the summer. We know it as a regulator plant, tiny and all as it might be, it is one of the most important plants we have growing here. Here Dottie, you can borrow my loupe," she said, unclipping the small brass magnifying glass from her necklace and handing it over to the very eager child. "There's a knack to it if you recall; hold it up to one of your eyes, keep both open, now rest the loupe on your hand, and rest your hand on your forehead, this will keep it steady and at the right distance from your eye," Nell explained. "The loupe will give you a great view while looking at the flower, make sure you don't have your back to the sun, you need its illumination, and get in as close as you can," Nell instructed. Dottie nodded and carefully lay on the ground organising herself in the correct position so that she could get the best and most comfortable view. Dottie carefully examined the plant as Nell had directed, and through that little magnifying glass, she could see what looked to her like a giant tree from some distant land. The fine details of its leaf structure and tiny flowers were revealed in powerful little lens and Dottie saw it was beautiful. She looked a little closer still and got a start as a magnified bug appeared just at the lower end of the stem. She giggled with delight. She moved on to the next little plant and she thought how she had never realised the beauty and wonder there was in this miniature world. And that was that—Dottie was hooked. "We learn from observation," Nell pronounced, and she could see Dottie was a true naturalist and keen to learn. Nell observed that Dottie was an excellent student and committed herself to teaching her everything she knew. She had to make sure from the start that she had the right student to pass her precious knowledge onto, and now that the fairies had also corroborated Dottie to be that person, Nell could begin guiding her into the ways of her ancient and mysterious craft. Nell invited her down to her cottage to show her all the plants she was nurturing there and to let Dottie's natural inquisitiveness grow organically. Soon Dottie was becoming a regular visitor to Nell's home, always being served a second dessert there too, which was to Dottie's delight of course, and Nell enjoyed the little girl's company. Nell liked to pass on her knowledge to Dottie and even in the garden she would point out a tree on the cottages' acre of ground, "this tree is so beneficial for healing peoples' ills, we use its leaves to keep everything clean around a wound or a sore on the body and it's leaf has great powers for healing generally, Dottie." Nell then made Dottie one of her favourites, a cinnamon and juniper drink,

"I've never tasted anything like it before, it's so yummy!" Nell was delighted.

"Well, you shall have to try out my rose hip and elderberry brew too, as it's full to the brim of good things to keep you hale and hearty, really something quite spectacular! The best time to pick the rose hips is always after the first frost comes, they are at their sweetest then," she said, delighted to have found someone with such a keen interest.

"Great Nell, next time I'll get my buckets ready for them when the blackberries are gone," Dottie said, thinking of the sweet new treats.

"I'll show you how to make my thyme syrup, great for keeping you healthy, and all the different ways of using other wild herbs, as well, the list is endless, my dear."

In the Autumn, Dottie's grandmother would bring her two grandchildren out to help in the walled garden to gather the apple harvest. Normally, her grandmother forbade the children from going in the orchard as Molloy kept his bees near the apple trees and she said she was afraid they might get stung. Of course, that never stopped Dottie, and she took no notice of her at all. She learnt the honeybees would not bother her if she did not bother them. She suspected that the wily old lady had used this as a ruse to keep her out of the orchard for fear she would be unable to resist the dangling fruits. She ventured in there any time she felt like it, to reach for an apple if one was ripe enough, and of course, she kept a good distance from the beehives as she certainly didn't fancy getting stung either.

CHAPTER 13

Seven and a Half

Dottie started school when she was four and a bit, after her initial reluctance to attending class, she was spending her late autumn, winter, and spring in the classroom, soaking up every detail she could extract from her schoolteachers. Nell waited till Dottie reached that magic age of seven and a half before she would put a most important question to her. She did this to allow the child the crucial decision, even at that young age, whether to explore her special abilities or not. When it comes to those with inherent magical gifts, it's up to each remarkable child to decide for themselves if they want to pursue those talents, and undertake the arduous journey to unlock, activate, and reach their full magical potential. Unbeknownst to Dottie, her own mother had at one time, at that special age of seven and a half, been singled out by the fairies; as a child who possessed 'the gift,' but she had decided to turn down that same offer of training and knowledge. She made up her mind that it was something she did not want to pursue, somehow knowing this was not her passion and chose instead a life of normality. For her mother, those innate gifts and magical powers faded as she grew, and she was quite happy to live out her childhood as a regular little girl. Over the years, whether by magic or not, she thought less and less about those abilities and, as with many childhood memories, wondered if such thoughts were more fantasy than fact.

The magic passes on from generation to generation, and the offer is made to each gifted child, until one is willing to take up the mantle.

Dottie was different to her mother in this respect; when the question was asked of her, she never hesitated. And yet, the moment seemed to occur in some timeless non-verbal space. Both Nell and Dottie smiled at each other, and so it was set in motion, a train of events that would change the course of the little girl's life henceforth.

Nell was there to guide Dottie and hone those talents that fate and inheritance had bestowed upon her. She encouraged her to get a more in-depth knowledge of her natural surroundings first and acted as guide, and interpreter, of the many wisdoms gleaned from the fairies.

"You have to know the basics first; the basics are the very foundation from which you can build upon," Nell would say. Dottie was learning fast, she spent two full summers playing with, and learning, from the fairy folk. She was introduced to so many of these wonder beings and loved each one as though they were her own little family. Each possessed their own individual talents; conveying insights to any problems Dottie might have with her understanding of the natural and magical world. They gladly revealed their great wealth of magical knowledge and treated her as one of their own.

Her mentor, Nell, was of an indeterminate age, and was clearly an older lady, but just how old Dottie could not even begin to guess. Sometimes, Dottie would ask,

"How old are you, Nell? If I am seven and a half years old," Dottie declared proudly, "so you must be at least double my age?" Nell hugged the little girl and laughed as she told Dottie that she was probably over a thousand years old, but could not be certain, she had lost count somewhere between her four hundred and eighth, and nine hundred and seventh birthdays.

"Honestly my dear," Nell said with utmost sincerity, "once you have eaten your five hundredth birthday cake, and blown out the myriad of coloured candles, one age feels very much like the next." Dottie looked at Nell for a moment, then a huge smile broke across Nell's face, and she burst out with mischievous laughter. "Well let me put it to you like this, I am a lot older than your mother and your father put together." On hearing this, Dottie's face lit up with amazement, then they both ended up laughing. In that laughter, it seemed that all the years between them just dissolved away. Dottie liked how Nell could put her at ease, she was a natural teacher who could impart her knowledge with intelligence, and when appropriate, with a sense of humour which could always hold the child's undivided attention.

"Nell is such a good teacher, so different to the masters and mistresses at school," thought Dottie. Surprisingly, Nell responded aloud,

"That's very kind of you to think that my dear, but remember, I have been doing this for many, many, many a year, so I have great respect for all educators." Dottie was mystified that Nell seemed to know what she was thinking, there was so much more to this marvellous old lady.

One chilly autumn evening, as they sat by the stove and sipped hot cocoa, Nell revealed that she was not from Dottie's realm. In fact, she was born in the realm of *Farne*. She explained that, aside from Dottie's realm, and Florestael where the fairies dwell, there were many other realms. Each one was full of endless wonders and other magical beings, but Nell chose to live in Dottie's world, the Earth, but known to magic folk as the realm of *Blusfloct*. Farne, where Nell was born and raised, was in a far-flung region; there, the giant and the small, lived in harmony. Her mother, Halava, still kept their family home there, and Nell visited her whenever she could. The folk of Farne had evolved into a very cooperative society, sharing as much magic and knowledge as possible. They discovered the many benefits of peace, after an ancient war between the giants and the small ended with both sides realising that their disagreements mattered far less than what was mutually beneficial. Over the eons, their realm became a model of harmonious co-existence for all the other realms, and so, in time, it became the graduating destination for all young apprentices of magic. Each Graduand had to go to Nell's realm to attend an inauguration ceremony on the Hill of Farne. When Nell herself graduated, she was nominated by the elders who sat on the *Council of Realms* (C.O.R.) to be the guardian of knowledge. She had been charged with its safekeeping and to pass on this knowledge only to those deemed worthy. Now she wanted to empower her new young protégé with the same breath of learning that she was gifted since that time. She knew Dottie was the ideal candidate for this timeless knowledge, and to be the beneficiary of all this wisdom. Knowing the fairies had recommended Dottie too, just confirmed her belief in this little girl. Dottie displayed all the empathy, joy, and that unquenchable thirst for knowledge, that garnered Nell's full attention. She would tutor her young student for as long as was required. Nell was sure that Dottie was the one.

Nell made teaching and learning fun, and Dottie absorbed everything rapidly; she had this insatiable appetite and thrived on everything Nell was imparting to her. Nell's first task was to bestow a comprehensive understanding of the power of plants to her student. Quite soon, she had advanced, and was now an adept scholar of the "Doctrine of Signatures," in botany and herbs. Over time, Dottie knew almost everything there was to know about what each plant did, how each plant had its own magical qualities and, in turn, was able to combine these with other ingredients to unlock their full potential and make them even more potent. In school she loved anything they taught her on biology and science, no matter how basic. Dottie also loved art and painting; she used this to make sense of all she was experiencing through her drawing. Her teacher just thought Dottie had a remarkable imagination, little realising much of Dottie's drawings of fairies and magic were, in fact, her recordings of real occurrences. Soon Dottie felt ready to strive for the powers Nell had told her about, keen to discover what she might achieve, but aware that these could not be attained without study, dedication, and practice. Dottie, although still a little girl, knew somehow that such powers would come at a price. Nell was not an enchantress in the traditional sense, but a natural sorceress; she had been born with her powers extant, and she recognised these same powers in Dottie. Nell explained exactly how these powers worked and what Dottie was capable of being.

"When the time is right, I am going to show you some magic, Dottie, so you must pay close attention," Nell announced. Dottie clapped her hands together gleefully on hearing this, as the fairies had already been showing her their magic, and this had filled her with curiosity; she wanted to know everything and literally begged Nell to show her.

"You're the best teacher in the whole wide world, please, please Nell, you have to show me some of your magic, pretty PLEASE! "Of course I will," said Nell with a smile, "but only one spell at a time, this is not something that can be rushed so look and learn," she said. But secretly, Nell was flattered by the "best teacher in the world" comment and said to herself "too right, too right indeed."

CHAPTER 14

The Cheromaack

Nell cleared her throat and then took on a serene appearance, she spoke in a mellifluous and authoritative tone; she seemed to connect with the very life force surrounding her, in tune with the rhythms of nature's time and space, a conduit from the roots of the Earth herself to the farthest away stars in the universe. In a flash, something materialised out of nowhere and enveloped her, and then she disappeared before Dottie's eyes, then reappeared behind her. Dottie was amazed, flabbergasted, could hardly speak, she was absolutely astounded at what had just taken place.

"I shall have to put this in simple terms, so basically, it's a magic cloak," Nell explained. "It's not made from any earthly material but is, in essence, an entity from an alternative reality known as the *Cheromaack*. In the process of becoming a practitioner of this magic, all new candidates complete an initiation ceremony, and as part of that process, the candidate must first be chosen by a Cheromaack. Then, should this happen, a wonderful symbiosis occurs, and that bond lasts for an eternity. The Cheromaack will become your guardian, only summoned when you need it, so the initial task you must undertake on your journey into the first stratum of magical realms, is to find, and be accepted, by your very own Cheromaack. She became a little concerned that Dottie did not say anything as she seemed to be in complete shock. Nell asked her if she was all right. Dottie was just stood there, eyes out on stalks, and her mouth had dropped open so wide a whole flock of starlings could have flown in. But soon she started to clap with glee, and jumped up and down chanting,

"Do it again Nell, do it again, do it again." Nell obliged by disappearing and reappearing again like the switching on of an electric light. Each time she reappeared, she laughed at Dottie's reaction of joy and in remembering how much fun it was for her. It brought back happy memories of when she got her very own Cheromaack many eons ago.

"I would love to have my very own magic cloak, Nell."

"Cheromaack," Nell corrected.

"Yes, sorry, I mean Cheromaack, the fairies showed me magic things when I first met and played with them, but then, they are fairies Nell, I never thought you could do this too! Boy, this is going to be so much fun. Are you sure I will be able to get my very own Cheromaack too?" Nell nodded in confirmation.

"Oh! I'd love that, I can hardly wait," Dottie said, thinking of the great excitement that lay ahead for her.

"I know some of this might all seem like great fun, and it is, but there are many times when this power brings with it great dangers, so you must never take it for granted or misuse it. The very moment that you do is the very moment that the power will no longer be yours to control, and the consequences can be dire." Nell explained, "Beware of its seductive powers and never get drawn in to use it for personal gain," she said firmly. Dottie just nodded, her mouth open, trying to take it all in, she did not fully understand what Nell was saying to her, but she knew that it was very important.

Over the next few weeks, Nell took the young sorceress-in-waiting on amazing journeys using her Cheromaack to transport them at impossible speeds. Dottie saw all the wonders of her world and more; she met all the ancients who as it transpired were great old friends of Nell's. She remembered some of their names but there was just too many. This was all so new, so strange, and so wonderful to Dottie. She was trying to make sense of it when really, it made no sense at all, so she was learning to just accept it as there was no real explanation. Gradually, and very carefully, Nell was exposing Dottie to the very outer edges of time and space, while allowing the youngster to absorb as much knowledge as she could take; without it ever being so much as to overwhelm her young charge. It pleased Nell greatly, that Dottie displayed all the same true qualities necessary of all who were to excel in sorcery; she was unafraid to ask questions, a true sign of natural intelligence. The power of flight was so liberating, Dottie felt she could go anywhere, and could see everything. These trips were far more eye-opening than any of the tales recounted by her parents' travels abroad. She would love to have told them about all the wonders that she had seen, but she knew they would never have believed her. It was all too magical for the ordinary folk in her life. It was a truly magical event every time. A fascinating fact she learned, was because Nell's Cheromaack had no past, present or future, it therefore had the power to transcend both time and space; because it had no temporal locus it belonged to nowhere and everywhere all at once.

CHAPTER 15

Farne

Nell and Dottie soared high through the skies and dipped down into far off places. One of the first places they went to visit was Petazsa, where Nell was born, in the realm of Farne. Nell explained to Dottie that each coloured band of the rainbow offered a different doorway into the other realms, with one more ornate than the next, and the Indigo band, was the doorway to her birthplace in the realm of Farne. Nell tried to explain just how and why the coloured bands allowed entry into each realm but even she struggled to make sense of it. There was a complex explanation about frequencies and resonances, but Nell saw the little girl's eyes glaze over and thought it best to leave that explanation for another time. Instead, Nell introduced Dottie to her mother, Halava, and they had tea on the lawn in front of her home. Halava asked Dottie if she was enjoying the scones to which Dottie replied,

"Oh yes, they're really yummy, thanks." Dottie looked over at Nell, who seemed a little ill at ease.

"Of course, baking keeps me busy, well, I may have had a little bit of magical help, of course, and my daughter brought me some blackberry jam months ago, so I would have it for visitors, I loved it when I lived on Blusfloct, and now I can't get enough of the bloody stuff!"

"Me too, I love blackberries. Can you not make your own jam here?" Dottie asked looking around at the luscious surroundings.

"Those delicious blackberries won't grow here at all you know, we just don't have the soil for it, not at all like Blusfloct," replied Halava.

Nell's mother was a very tall woman and very beautiful, she had the most amazing skin, she had a golden glow about her that Dottie could not quite put her finger on. She seemed a bit impatient with Nell, Dottie observed. "I can grow everything here but not the plants from your realm. You know dearie, they've named a dessert after me back in Blusfloct, eternal life and all that, she trailed off – looking over at Nell. "I could do with Nell's help back here now and again, but she always seems too busy to visit her old mum," she said, looking down at little Dottie, giving her a conspiratorial wink, while giving Nell another quick sideways glance.

"Oh, you know I get here when I can, MOTHER, I can't always be here all of the time," she replied, sounding somewhat irked.

"Yes, yes, you're far too busy in Blusfloct to visit, I know, I know – anyway who's for more tea?"

Farne was a place of endless wonders and such friendly people, Dottie felt so welcomed in all the places Nell brought her to. She soon grew used to soaring high at great speeds as they flew through the ether. Dottie observed the way that the Cheromaack was able to carry them both with such ease and comfort; how safe it made her feel and how it seemed to exude this wonderful aroma, like fresh honeysuckle. Prior to embarking on this amazing adventure, Dottie had thought the wider world was everything her mother and father had told her about. Now, on her travels with Nell, she discovered worlds within worlds that were breathtakingly beautiful and terrifically exciting. She had always thought the farm was her entire world but now she could see that it was only just the beginning of her story. Dottie was still very young and so when her mother would call her in for her tea, Nell would ensure that the little girl was safely back home each evening.

"No matter where we go, I'll *always* have you home in time for your tea, and that's a promise" Nell stated warmly. Even if at first, it appeared to the little girl that she and her wise mentor had been at great distances from home, and had spent, what seemed to Dottie, like hours, even days, away on adventures, in the blink of an eye, she would suddenly be back just outside the farm, as if no time had passed at all. Home – safe. After the first few trips, Dottie would be back sitting in the kitchen with her hair standing on end, generally looking a bit dishevelled, and in a mild state of culture-shock. But after going on a few more such trips, she was soon accustomed to this strange and wonderful way of travelling, she could hardly wait and looked forward to each new flight. Once back home, seated and warming her toes by the powder-blue coloured Rayburn stove, she would be humming contentedly to herself while staring into its flickering flames. Dottie would sip her tea as her grandmother opened the stove door to add a few more sods of turf and ignoring Dottie who was happily munching away on some buttered toast with gooseberry jam and dreaming of her next adventure with Nell.

CHAPTER 16

The Spell and The Council of Realms

O ver the next few months Nell was able to test Dottie's abilities and each time she passed with flying colours. For her next most important task, Dottie was to prepare her first magical potion; being of the correct age, it was now her time to make up such a potion. This would begin her journey towards becoming a qualified sorcerer, and for her to be able to realise her full potential. A prescribed sequence of events needed to be followed to the letter. All of Nell's preparations with her student were leading up to this moment, it was now time to pass on those very special magical recipes to Dottie, one that was passed on in ancient times by the little people of *Bratstanwolf* in the realm of Farne. Once the magical child had mastered gathering all the ingredients on their own, they would then begin the process of being indoctrinated into The C.O.R. in a ceremony on the Hill of Farne. There was a very long tradition of assembling on the hill, officially greeting, heartily supporting, and welcoming all the new recruits into the magic sphere. To be able to access and pass through the magical doorways in the rainbow, Dottie also needed to be of the right character and morals to attend her own inauguration ceremony, and to be permitted to claim her first spell. But most important of all, was to be worthy of acquiring Cheromaack of her very own. This was one of the oldest spells in this, or any realm, and had to be mastered; once achieved, the child sorceress could then master anything and would continue to grow in power using this esoteric knowledge. But this came with its own weighty set of responsibilities, which Dottie soon learned. A cornerstone of magic was one must never use their magic for personal gain; this rule was paramount, because if a spell was ever misused, then that spell would be rendered useless for evermore. Furthermore, no one in any of the other realms would be able to use it ever again; it would be lost for eternity. Therefore, it was vital that no charlatans ever got past this important first step. It was in everyone's best interests to meet and make sure the young ones understand fully the ramification of their powers; while they had a natural talent, they had yet to learn, focus, and to control their gifts, for if they misused anger or any other negative emotion, and let it seep into their spellmaking, then it would only cloud their own judgements, and all would suffer the loss of that misused spell.

"Spell right, spell is bright; spell wrong, spell is gone!" was how Nell would explain it. "It is policed by the magic itself, and while no one knows exactly how that part of the process works, they just know it works, and they know to never stray from that dictum." Nell went on to explain one of the magic sphere's losses which little Dottie would be able to understand, "Legend has it, that once upon a time, a naïve sorcerer had misused the ability to speak with reptiles; having become angry that his older brother had broken his magical golden lyre, he had cast a spell on a grass snake to slither up inside his brother's tunic and bite him on the bottom. So, what may have seemed an inconsequential act by a young sorcerer, had now taken the gift of speaking *Reptilinia* away from all forever." Nell noticed a tear coming from Dottie's eye and asked, "What's upsetting you, little one? I would love to have been able to speak with a grass snake, but now I just feel so sorry for all those snakes, and lizards, who can't enjoy a simple chat over a cup of tea and scone with us anymore." Nell hugged her little friend and laughed.

"It's no great loss, my child, reptiles make very poor conversationalists." Dottie was nodding seriously as Nell spoke and she swore she would never misuse her powers for any sort of greedy or mean things. Dottie thought of her sister, Viola, who always seemed to be angry at her for doing something or saying something in conversation, "Well, then my sister could never do this as she always gets so angry with me when I ask her for help with my maths homework." Viola doubted everyone and everything she could not understand, whereas Dottie trusted Nell, and instinctively believed what she was saying, gaining so much from this wisdom, choosing to live in the light. Whereas Viola, would never trust anyone, or believe in anything, and therefore chose to live in the darkness.

CHAPTER 17

The Magical Ingredients

By the time of the pink moon, when the sun was in Aquarius, it was organised for Dottie to begin her first magical adventure. Nell would be by her side to guide her young apprentice and prepare her for the inauguration ceremony. For Dottie to transition from apprentice to practitioner, she would have to collect nine special ingredients from nine different realms. These discrete ingredients, had to be gathered at a set moment in the astrological calendar, unique to each realm, which would then in turn release their magical individual qualities. Not only did Dottie have the task of collecting the ingredients from these realms, but also for her first spell to be magical, she had to collect each specific ingredient at the same time on the same day.

"Nell, how will I be fast enough to get all the ingredients at the same time?" Dottie asked with some trepidation.

"Well now dear, everything's possible when you believe in the magic of it all. Believe each realm starts at the same time when you enter them, that's the magic working for you, you'll begin at the start, every child begins with their home realm; your quest shall begin here in Blusfloct. You will acquire your first ingredient, and so begins the process. Then, in the second realm, as soon as you enter it, then you will find it is at the exact same time as the realm you first started with. And so on and so forth; it all makes sense when you begin, otherwise it just sounds senseless. It's best to be brave, take the first step, and before you know it, you're underway. The one advantage of time behaving in this fashion, is that no matter how long it might take, its exactly the right amount of time it should take, and you will always be home in time for tea. The belief in doing it, and that belief in yourself, conquers all doubts, this is what magic is, and as I always say, when in doubt, take one task at a time. Remember, the smallest ant can climb the highest mountain because they believe they can. No one is there to tell them any different, and so, they just take one tiny step at a time, and before you know it, they are at the summit," said Nell, with a knowing smile. Dottie nodded and chose to believe, as she thought it made perfect sense, she need not worry at all.

Dottie was the kind of child who took her time over tasks and liked to get them done just so. "Now, I have a present for you, this is for passing all my classes and learning so well, it will help with your next stage too," Nell explained, as she presented Dottie with a little gift all wrapped up in golden wrapping paper and tied with a lovely pink bow. Her eyes lit up and she hugged and thanked Nell while proceeding to open the gift. It was a little magical golden scissors for cutting plants at angles and her own golden loupe on a golden chain, both with her name engraved on them.

"Oh, great, thank you," said an underwhelmed Dottie. She had hoped that it would have been chocolate or some other yummy, sweet treat, not a pair of old scissors. While Dottie did her best to hide her disappointment, Nell could read Dottie's thoughts. Nell gave her a disapproving look, and muttered, "Master this and soon you'll be able to have all the chocolate you wish.

What was that Nell, I didn't quite hear you properly?" But Nell said it was nothing, instead she moved on to explain why they were such important tools,

"Now, in your own realm, you have to pick a plant, we call it a starter or control plant in our business, at precisely twelve noon on that day, it has to be cut at an angle of exactly thirty-three degrees, these 'old' scissors will work this angle out for you, but first, you must turn around in a complete circle and bow to greet each of the meridian points." She demonstrated this by standing on one leg and spun around in a full circle, greeting each point, and then bending down to pretend to cut an imaginary plant. Dottie laughed at the sight of Nell spinning around, Nell laughed with her, and agreed it did look quite funny, then continued; "And then you will take the scissors and cut the stalk of the plant just so and place it in a mixture of apple cider vinegar, cod liver oil, and a cat's whisker. Then, let it soak overnight. This will be the only plant we require from your realm for this spell Dottie." Nell explained that an elder had to accompany the chosen gifted child so she could pick the other ingredients from other realms but that she would not be allowed to intervene in the act of cutting. Nell had been selected by the C.O.R. as most suitable and, more importantly, precisely attuned to Dottie's magical aura. "We shall be going on an adventure the day after tomorrow, Dottie, and I shall have you back by tea; I never want your mother to worry.

Oh, great, I just love going on adventures Nell.

All will be revealed…tomorrow… now, get a good night's sleep and I shall see you here tomorrow at eleven forty-five am precisely, so don't be late.

I usually have to help out with some kitchen chores for my gran first thing in the morning," Dottie said in an upbeat tone. "I'll race down here as soon as I'm finished. Oh, I can hardly wait," Dottie exclaimed, full to the brim with excitement.

"Of course, you'll be eager, and that's only to be expected little one, now don't forget to bring a jam jar, and label it yours so Molloy doesn't use it for something else, and a lid of course. In the jar pour two parts cod liver oil to one-part apple cider vinegar, then close the lid tight. I also want you to bring me one cat's whisker, not plucked mind, she said as she wagged her finger at Dottie, "but one that the cat has left fall and is happy for you to have. All the rest will be revealed tomorrow my dear," Nell instructed.

The Gathering

The next morning as Dottie got up, she looked out of the window over the front lawn; it was such a lovely morning. She noticed something move near the inner gate and saw a lovely brown fox crossing the path, she tried to get Viola to come and see,

"Viola, VIOLA, look – a fox! A FOX!! Come see. Ohhh, he is just so lovely.

Shut up Dottie, stop lying. Will you ever just stop making things up? Just leave me alone, will you?!" Viola exclaimed and would not budge from under the covers. Not even to see whether, or not, Dottie was telling the truth. Viola just assumed the worst of her little sister every time.

"Well, I DID see the fox, and I don't care if you believe me or not." However, Viola was snoring loudly, so Dottie turned on her heels, stomped heavily across the wooden floor, and slammed the bedroom door shut. She could hear Viola's startled reaction and that made Dottie giggle. Viola was never going to change her view of her younger sister, she never believed anything she said and always calling her a liar. Viola seemed to have an inherent resistance to dreaming and creativity, whereas Dottie loved to dream, to experience the joys of life and to learn.

Around eleven o' clock that morning Dottie met Nell in the garden. Nell was checking out the regulator plant to see if it could cut it yet.

"Everything has to be just-so for harvesting and this plant is now ready. Now is the perfect time for this plant to be cut," she thought to herself. "It's the one that gives you the start in your quest for flight," Nell exclaimed, sensing the excitement building now. "Dottie, we cannot start your journey to obtain any other plant or flower without this very first one; it is the key that unlocks it all, once you begin, the process must be continued on to completion. When you have gathered all the other plants for your first spell, then, and only then, you will be introduced to your very own Cheromaack and, through it, gain the power of flight."

"My very own flying cloak…. how smashing."

"Yes dearie, but do try not to call it a cloak, the Cheromaack are very touchy about that word so never use it when talking of them… and never, ever, refer to them as being capes. As the other ingredients and plants cannot grow here, we will be spending a good proportion of our time travelling between the other realms. When the time is twelve noon in the day, begin by turning around once anticlockwise to unlock the genesis of the spell, then everything will be primed, and events start to take on a momentum all of their own. As it is now approaching that time, my dear, take a deep breath and then, when you're ready, you can cut the first plant."

Dottie remembered her instructions and turned around in a circle on one leg, bowing to each meridian point. Then, at precisely the right moment, she cut the plant at exactly the right location on its stem, at the required angle, guided by her magic scissors of course. So began the collection of each constituent part of the potion for her ceremony. She could hardly contain her excitement at the prospect of it all. Nell, ever watchful of her charge, calmed her down,

"Well done, that was perfect, but you must try not to rush to the next moment. Take your time, patience is the key; we need to immerse the plant in the vinegar and oil mixture for now."

In her pocket Dottie had a cat's whisker. She saw one of the farm cats called, "Benskin," dozing in the garden the day before relaxing in the afternoon sunshine. Dottie noticed a long thin white object, or what at first, she thought was string, on his shiny black fur as he snoozed in the long grass. His tail twitching casually as he dozed. She went over to him, she never wanted to pull a whisker out of the poor unsuspecting creature's face anyway, so was delighted when she went to stroke him only to discover a whisker from his face had shed and landed on his coat while he was cleaning himself. Dottie, remembering she had the whisker, took it out of her pocket to show to Nell,

"I got the cat's whisker too, what is that for?" Dottie announced excitedly.

"Goodness only knows," said Nell, blowing it briskly from her hand and leaving Dottie rather puzzled.

The lid was then screwed back on and left to stand in one of the greenhouses in the garden overnight. They labelled it *Dottie's Mixture*. After that, Nell and Dottie had a nice long lunch on the lawn behind Nell's cottage. The sun was unusually warm for this time of year, so Nell and Dottie sat in the shade of an old leafy tree; watching clouds float overhead and seeing what they formed into.

"I see a tiger," declared Dottie.

"I see a pirate ship on a rough sea," said Nell. This was another reason why Dottie loved Nell's company so much. She was the only adult she knew who loved to while away the hours cloud-watching and would always see the most fantastical shapes.

They passed away the afternoon happily, and as it was getting near half past five, Nell was aware that Dottie needed to be getting back home again.

"Part one done, now, you need to go home to your mother for now. I want you to go to bed early and get your sleep for tomorrow's adventure, you're going to need your rest."

That night, as instructed, Dottie went to bed early. She was having the most wonderful dreams; vivid colours surrounded her. In her dreams, she floated through the rainbow and flew in the crisp fresh air, speeding, soaring, and falling, and then waking up with a start. She fell back to sleep again, but this time, she went in through a different door of the rainbow. She felt suddenly cold, and all the colours turned to grey. An air of menace surrounded her, a frightening feeling which caused her wake up. She felt scared and pulled her little toy bear, Teddy, close to her. Teddy was a very special friend; she had him since she was an infant in her cot and always slept with him snuggled next to her. Hugging Teddy tight, she instantly felt cosy and safe again and nodded off into a very deep slumber indeed. Teddy was always there to keep her safe.

The next morning, once again, Dottie could not get out the door fast enough. After her breakfast, which she had wolfed down, she shoved back her chair and dashed out of the kitchen,

"BYE GRAN!" she shouted as she charged toward the back door.

"Don't you dare slam that – " but her grandmother's warning was cut short by the thunderous sound of the back door shutting hard against its frame. Her grandmother just rolled her eyes up to heaven, "That girl will be the death of me," then, with a deep sigh, she went back to kneading dough for the day's bread and was soon lost in the process once more. Within minutes, Dottie had raced down to Nell's cottage and rushed in the back door and into the kitchen.

"Well, good morning, dear, did you sleep well?" Nell asked, with a smile.

"I did, except in one of my dreams I went through another door of the rainbow, it was all dark and gloomy, with big metal doors, it was really scary. I heard the cry of the banshee coming from the other side of the doorway, and then it opened slowly. I could see this bony pasty white hand with very long thin fingers, and I felt I couldn't stop myself from moving closer and closer towards it. Then, suddenly it grabbed me, it was trying to drag me through, that was when I woke up feeling really frightened, Nell." Dottie shuddered at the memory of her dream.

"Wonderful," said Nell. "That is excellent my dear, it sounds like your dream took you to doorway of the realm, *Sherastnorth*. That shows how in tune you are becoming and how sensitive you are. But don't worry Dottie, we won't venture in there until you've gained all your spells and full magic powers. Until then, you would do well to stay clear of that awful place, even in your dreams my child."

"It's ok Nell, I had Teddy to protect me and then I had a great night's sleep in the end," Dottie exclaimed happily.

"That's great dear, Teddy is a talisman and will always be there for you to guard your dreams, so you should never feel frightened," Nell said with a wry smile. "It's only because you don't fully understand it yet, but once you learn all about it, you will know how to deal with it, and you won't be frightened then. Knowledge will always show you the way out of the darkness. Come along, it's nearly mid-day, we must gather the potion from the greenhouse and be on our way. The other realms are always a day behind the time of a sorcerer-in-training's realm, and today all will match up with the same time at noon with the rest of the plants to be collected. All of the ingredients must be gathered and mixed in with the control plant, by the time of the ceremony for you which takes place on the hill at noon today."

"I still don't quite understand how we can ever collect all the ingredients AND also attend the ceremony all at the same time Nell, but I guess magic will find a way.

Yes Dottie, like I said before, it makes senseless sense or what I like to call *Ominous Logic* so best not to try to think about it too much, go along with it and all will be as it should."

Then, with an eager smile on her face, Dottie declared, "Ready? Steady? Let's go!"

Nell summoned her Cheromaack, and they took off once more to gather more magical plants and flowers

The next ingredient they were to collect was a mythical plant known as *Vin*. The flower has bright, orange-coloured petals and a white centre, a type of orange daisy, like the daisy in Blusfloct. But, unlike regular daisies, Vin has a square flower with a pearlescent centre and has great magical qualities. Vin is only found by going through the doorway, on the yellowy-green band of the rainbow.

"This land is a great source for all of our magic, it's known as *Vilshoct* to us realm-dwellers.

It's so quiet in here, Nell," said a slightly awe-struck Dottie. "Why yes it has always been a very peaceful place, even the animals living here hardly make a sound. This realm was allowed to be completely covered with all the plants and herbs that naturally grow here. No land has been built on or used to grow anything else; only what grows here naturally. It has been this way back since the beginning of magic. We all respect this, and even the dark magicians require the unique plants of Vilshoct from time to time, so even they would never attempt to alter this realm. There is a great fear of all practitioners of losing the realm's most precious plant, Vin. In order to protect it, an equilibrium has developed between good and bad," Nell explained. "In Vilshoct, a natural truce occurs between both good and bad; even if we cross each other's paths here, we must greet each other politely lest our negative energy towards each other damages the delicate Vin."

They walk onwards and, in no time at all, they found some Vin growing in a clearing, Dottie was guided to only pick the Vin with her left hand, and it must be pulled and not cut, "this is the only way to release its powers for good," she advised, it would be very wise for Dottie to always remember this one. Vin is the flower that turns on the relationship between the magic that you desire and want to hold onto, it is used in all magic spells everywhere," she proclaimed, and is a vital component to everything you shall ever do again."

"That's good to know," Dottie nodded thoughtfully.

"It's absolutely everywhere in this magical land, and all the magic in all the realms require it as a base to their potions," Nell said knowingly. "Place the whole flower in the potion mixture and make sure it is all coated with the vinegar and oil mix before we move along."

As they were doing this, Nell could hear someone approaching, and she sensed it was not a good energy, so she hushed Dottie up and they hid in the deep undergrowth behind some highly scented bushes. From this position, it was then easy to see who or what was passing by.

"Nell, I thought you said it was safe here?" she whispered.

"Well yes, except for one exception; *Trenics*, they are dangerous, they may have three heads, but they barely have one brain cell between them and could chase us or harm the Vin with their stupidity, so it's always best to hide first and see who it is," Nell replied, peeping through the bushes. Sure enough, she was right to be cautious. Dottie had never seen such a being before, it had three heads on the one body. The creature appeared to be arguing with itself,

"Well, you're not going to take all the glory for getting this for Shirda, she will just be rewarding me, and not you so there" one head said to the others.

"Hey, I was the one who spotted it first' said another of the heads.

"Yes, but you would not have recognised it if it wasn't for me," said the third head.

"*Greana*?" said the first head, "I KNEW it was Greana the moment I saw it, you thought it was *Eugrah*, but I knew right away it was Greana," the first head argued. Suddenly, the creature stopped its argument and started to sniff the air. All three of its noses twitched as the Trenic's heads looked around, searching….sniffing. It paused just by the bush where Nell and Dottie were hiding. It scrunched up all six of its eyes and wrinkled its noses, and for a moment, it appeared like it had a revelation, then just as suddenly, it shrugged its shoulders and walked away continuing to argue with itself.

"That was lucky," said Nell, "they probably were unable to smell our scent because of this aromatic *Senci* bush we hid in. Thank goodness for that, dear, those Trenics might have three noses, but they haven't one good brain between them. Take them seriously child, they are the worst when they catch you. They are always on the lookout for some prize or other to please Shirda, and we would have probably gone into her dungeons if they caught us," Nell said with a shiver. "One thing I am sure of is that when Shirda's Trenics are sent into Vilshoct to gather Greana, then she's up to something, and I shall have to make a report of this to the council.

"Who is Shirda?" Dottie asked.

"She's one of the seven bad rulers of Sherastnorth," replied Nell.

"Is Sherida very scary, Nell?" Dottie asked with concern.

"She is the ringleader, but the other six are just as bad as her, if not worse, one trying to outdo the other to gain power over the dwellers of their realm. Once they achieve that, then they tend to expand outward, and turn their attentions on the other realms. They want to rage wars in an attempt to overpower us all you see; we have always kept an eye on them to make sure that they don't get too powerful. If that were to happen, then I dread to think of the consequences for us all. But you don't have to worry yourself about all that for now. I shall fill you in with more detail when you're a little older, plenty of time for that," said Nell, with a kindly smile. "Now, we must be moving along."

"It sounds really scary, Nell, but I think it would be good for me to know all about them after my ceremony," Dottie said, eager to know more about these bad rulers.

"You have so many questions, and that is a good thing, but right now we must focus on the task in hand and collect the ingredients for your ceremony potion," said Nell.

"This next plant is protected by a great dragon, it is very rare indeed, it is the golden fruit from *The Great Tree of Quantock* that you must pick. Remember, it is a magic fruit, and while it might seem large at first, it will fit into the mix without any fuss at all, just remember that," reassured Nell.

"But what about the dragon, won't he be cross Nell?" Dottie asked nervously.

"Oh, he won't bite, he won't let just anybody pick the fruit, but he will take to you, Dottie, straight away, and of that I'm quite sure," answered Nell, with a reassuring chuckle. As she laughed, Dottie noticed that Nell seemed to be getting younger by the second, she wondered if it was a trick of the light in this realm or was this yet another of Nell's magical abilities?

"To Quantock!" Nell declared, and in a flash they were off.

Drackon the Dragon

In an instant they were standing before the red colour band of the rainbow, and on this occasion, they had to knock ever-so politely on the large, and rather ornate reddish-brown doorway. A little man came to the door to greet them. Dottie said hello but couldn't help noticing what a small little fellow he was, not at all like a fairy he was just like a mini person, all his features were in perfect proportion, she was amazed,

"How is he able to open such a large door," she thought, he laughed and graciously welcomed them inside.

"Good morning to you Nell, and your young friend, you're both very welcome to Quantock. And who might this young lady be that's accompanying you on such a fine morning as this?" he asked and winked at Nell. A smiling Nell then introduced Dottie to Virgil. She explained that he was the guardian of the red doorway. He had settled there centuries ago and was originally from the realm of Farne. Nell and Virgil were very old friends, and laughed freely, making Dottie feel very welcome indeed.

"Anyway, come in, come in, I think Drackon will be very pleased to see Dottie and yourself. Come on over to The Great Tree and I shall introduce you to him myself." Drackon was not visible as they were approaching the biggest tree that Dottie had ever seen and could not fathom how she was going to pick one of its giant fruits at all,

"That is the biggest quince tree I've ever seen," Dottie whispered tentatively.

"Now Dottie, I would like you to meet Drackon," Virgil said, and gestured to nothing in particular. But, by magic of course, a great and beautiful red, green, and blue dragon appeared. He was bigger than The Great Tree itself. He had beautiful jade green eyes, the colours on his body were every shade of green, every shade of red and every shade of blue. Although his size was fearsome, Dottie was not in the least bit frightened and actually felt safe with him. He spoke with a beautiful warm voice and greeted all, nodding to Nell who he already knew,

"Good morning, and who do we have here? Who do I have the great pleasure of meeting this fine morning?" he said with a dignified, cultured air, putting his head down close to inspect the little girl.

"My dear Drackon, this is my friend Dottie, she's in preparation for her ceremony and is here to ask you if she could pick one of the beautiful fruits from The Great Tree."

"Hello Mr Drackon, very pleased to meet you," she said with a curtsy.

"Well, and I am very honoured that you should come and meet me my child. Oh, isn't she ever so polite?" he said, seeming to glow with a golden hue.

"Can you really breathe fire, Mr Drackon?" asked Dottie with a nervous giggle.

"Dottie," hissed Nell, "you should never ask a dragon if he can breathe fire." Sensing his old friend's discomfort Drackon interjected

"That's perfectly fine, Nell, why of course I can child, but I only do so if I feel threatened," he said seriously, then a huge smile cracked across his snout and he laughed; a big smoky laugh, sending shockwaves around the tree and beyond. Taking is his awesome presence; the very thought of such a massive and powerful creature feeling threatened by anyone, or anything, was so impossible to imagine it was hilarious. Nell started to laugh also, albeit it a little nervously, then Virgil and Dottie joined in, each one triggering even more raucous laughter in the other. It was good that Drackon was in such a jocular mood; as Virgil and Nell both knew the devastation he was capable of should he ever lose his temper. Both having witnessed his awesome destructive power at first hand a very long time ago. "Now dear," said Nell, "you will have to ask Drackon politely if you can pick one of the golden fruits from The Great Tree for your potion." Dottie cleared her throat and put the question to him. "Dear Mr Drackon, would you allow me to pick one of your beautiful golden quinces for my ceremony today?" Dottie asked shyly.

"Oh, she is absolutely adorable, Nell. Now firstly, you must call me Drackon, I can't be doing with all that 'mister' carry-on, and if you climb up upon my claw here, I will take you to one of my most perfectly ripened fruits to help give you the best potion for your ceremony.

"Oh, that would be lovely, thank you so much Drackon," Dottie exclaimed, beaming with happiness. She climbed up and onto the dragon's claw; his skin felt soft and velvety the touch, with downy like fur, and short feathers, and not at all scaly, as it first appeared. He gently brought her to the top of The Great Tree, she could see a huge golden fruit in front of her.

"It's as big and bright as the moon," Dottie perused, but didn't hesitate, and reached out to pick it. Suddenly, it was only the size of her little hand, and fitted perfectly into the mixture. Virgil looked at Nell with a knowing smile. He then left them for a little while; only to come back moments later carrying quince tea and sweet little cakes on a delicately painted porcelain tray. They all sat for a while catching up on everything that had been happening in the realm of Quantock. Virgil filled Nell in on the goings on of the place since her last visit, Drackon asked Dottie if she would like to take a trip with him around the realm, so with a little help from Nell, she was able to climb onto the back of his neck and she held on tight as he took off for a quick tour around Quantock.

It was a wild and rocky place with mountainous active volcanoes stretching as far as the eye could see. But it was not without areas of lush vegetation; with plants and trees that looked amazing to Dottie with their colourful foliage. More dragons were flying about, but Drackon was by far the largest one. "I am considered the king of the dragons here in Quantock, my dear, and all look to me to protect everything you see around you. I have been doing so since I first knew that it was my destiny. We get the occasional challenge to who is in charge, and other bad realm-dwellers sometimes come to try and take all the precious things that we have in our realm."

"Oh, like the fruit from The Great Tree, Drackon?" Dottie asked.

"Well, exactly my dear child, that would be just one of our great treasures," the dragon said mysteriously.

"It is probably because you are so kind, others might try to take advantage of that," Dottie suggested.

"That might be so, that might be so," said a thoughtful Drackon. "But you see, I wasn't always the happy dragon you see before you, sometimes I could be really mean, you see, I used to lose my temper a lot, and lose all control, that was until I was saved by a little girl very much like you Dottie. She was wise too, as you are, and showed me how to use my great power for good. Surprisingly, I found I liked it far better than being mean; being mean takes a lot of energy and I don't think I would still be here had that kind and clever girl not shown me a different way. Why you could say that I would have burnt out."

They flew the rest of the tour around Quantock in a comfortable complete silence, it was all so wonderful Dottie thought, and the silence with Drackon was so refreshing. The views from on high were breath-taking to witness, words could not even begin to describe it. In time, they returned to where they had begun their flight and Drackon set Dottie back down near Nell. The little girl was so excited and happy she could hardly contain herself,

"Oh, my goodness, what a flight! I've just been on the most amazing journey with Drackon. I can't quite believe it really happened, what a treat. There's no way my sister is ever going to believe me, she didn't even believe me when I told her I saw a lovely brown fox at the gate, what are the chances that she would every believe me if I told her I went flying on the back of a dragon? That was truly amazing, Drackon, your realm is so magical and…and…. fantastic," she said using the most expressive word she could think of.

"Why, thank you my dear," he responded, winking a giant eye at Nell, and giving out a tremendous loud and sooty belly laugh. They all had to hold on to something so as not to be blown away by the sheer force of his roar, then after all was calm again, they had a further chat about her upcoming ceremony. Drackon announced, "If I can be of any service at all in the future, do not hesitate in coming to see me straight away, Dottie, " he insisted.

After a while, they bid their farewells, and moved on, until they found themselves at the front of the next doorway. "I don't know why I was so nervous of meeting Drackon now; dragons are not scary at all."

"Well, you just saw him on his best behaviour today but trust me you do not ever want to see his bad side. It is only still beautiful here because of his love for Quantock. Only for him, it would have been invaded and destroyed eons ago. Were he, and his dragon comrades, to use their full powers in anger, the entire realm would be nothing but ash and cinders. It is his example of quiet restraint that all the other dragons follow," Nell explained. "Now ready yourself Dottie, we have more work to do."

The Land Where The Fairies Dwell

Nell pushed once on the door and said, "So here we are now, outside the entrance to the next realm, known as Florestael; and of course, this is our dear friend, Mabel's home."

"Oh great," said Dottie, "can we call to see her and play for a while?" she asked gleefully.

"On any other day, yes, but today we are on a quest, and must stay focused. Anyway, she is very busy at this time of year; the fairies have their annual congress, and it's strictly by invitation only. So now, back to your quest, and the plant here that you will be looking for is called, *Floris*. They are recognised by their wonderful scent, and have a little white flower, mind you, all the flowers here in this realm are white, but this is the tiniest little one of all. Now Dottie, you will need your loupe at the ready to see this one close-up," Nell exclaimed, matter-of-factly.

This beautifully ornate doorway through the green-blue band of the rainbow was the entrance to Florestael. The whole place had a greenish-blue glow about it, everything was whiter-than-white, even the foliage was white. The landscape was reminiscent of a chill winter's day back home for Dottie, so much so, that she believed she felt cold.

"I should have brought a hat and gloves and maybe a coat too," she mumbled to herself.

Dottie set to work with the little magnifying glass looking down to see what flowers were there, as she was carefully trying to spot the flower, a tiny little hummingbird was busy hovering about and around the flowers carpeting the ground beneath her feet,

"There is a little hummingbird here, look it is the most magical little thing ever, it's so perfect and so pretty," she proclaimed. Nell then had a look, as it was a sight to behold,

"That's a hummingbird moth, Dottie." They observed its little eyes; so calm while at the same time, its tiny wings were going at great speeds. Dottie watched it going about its business, busy sucking the nectar from the little flowers. Nell explained, "this realm has the tiniest of everything here, for this is the place of the fairies after all. You cannot hurt things here by stepping on them as everything here has magic, they are a collective of magic and, although it looks serene, it is one of the most powerful of realms."

Dottie was mesmerised by this new place, and she was amazed by all she had seen so far. She was practically blinded by the white glare of the place as her eyes still had not adjusted to its light.

"Mabel and the others are so lucky to live in a place like this, it is truly a sight to behold," she gasped.

"She is, but you should see it when it is in full bloom at the height of their summer, it's an absolute wonder, I know Mabel can't wait for you to visit, and you can do all these wonderful things after you have completed your ceremony. So, come along now, let's get on with the flower gathering.

This is the only time of year that the Floris flower grows; the one we seek from this realm. I'm sure you'll become a regular visitor here," Nell announced with a smile. Dottie nodded, and with the aid of her loupe, she picked the tiniest white Floris flower and put it into her container. Nell explained, "This flower is one of the most potent when using it for spells, we'll be coming back to this realm quite frequently, as you'll need it for making many of your potions."

"Brrrr, it is so cold here," Dottie said. However, looks were deceptive and soon she realised it was not in the least bit cold there at all, but a pleasantly mild climate.

As they journeyed on Nell explained to Dottie that it only appeared cold because of the white colour of the surroundings that tricked the mind into believing it was cold. "Another interesting fact about this realm of Florestael is that it is also inhabited by *Sirolls*. They spend their time here pretending to be fairies, they cannot not fly at all, and are not very small, but they are very slim and have all the other appearances of fairies. They have very little magic, none to speak of really, except the knowledge of getting to Florestael," Nell explained. "They just like the peace of this realm and gravitate to that feeling of calm. They always love falling asleep once they are cosy. They have all the behavioural aspects of cats back on Blusfloct. They're friendly, but they like to keep to themselves, and enjoy the food that grows all around Florestael. They'll graze all day, then sleep in warm caves, or in the long grasses," she explained.

"But I haven't seen any Sirolls?" said Dottie.

"Oh, they are here alright, Dottie, don't you worry, once they're asleep it's near impossible to see them as they blend in with their surroundings," said Nell, recounting her previous encounters with the Siroll. "They are as adept as a Madagascan gecko at camouflage, and it's easiest for them to come here now with its full-on dazzling white light. They sleep all the time. They're amazing beings really, I'm sure you'll meet them another time. Come now, we must be gone, onwards and upwards..." and with a sweep of her Cheromaack they were off.

CHAPTER 21

Swimming in the Clouds

As they appeared at the next entrance, Nell explained, "Now Dottie, this next realm has a very, very red, red flower, it survives by floating in the wind and you have to be fast to catch one, it's not grounded at all, nothing here is." They stood just outside the yellowy-orange colour band of the rainbow; the door was quite plain compared to the others that Dottie had observed thus far. They went through, and then the door disappeared behind them.

"This realm is known to all as *Mact*," Nell announced, floating, and hovering above Dottie, as they both bobbed up and down in the ether. "The law of gravity does not apply here Dottie, but don't worry, you'll soon get the hang of it…think of it as swimming in air!" There were cumulus clouds of various red dusty hues, everything was floating around them including Dottie and Nell around each other. Dottie started to enjoy herself and played in this most unusual place. She adapted fast, and soon she could literally fly rings around Nell. They both laughed and enjoyed the fun of weightlessness. Dottie began to feel there were others joining in with their fun, although she could not see anyone around them. There was a joyous feeling of merriment coming from all about her. She sensed others joining in, and playing around her, and she felt spinning sensations on either side of her. Nell spoke softly to Dottie and reiterated that she had to be fast to catch this red flower. "It only ever has one leaf attached to its stem and while it resembles a rose from Blusfloct, it is not related to the rose at all, and magic folk know it as *Bilnd*.

"Do folk live here? Dottie asked, "It feels like there are others around me, but I cannot see anyone. I can hear them; can you hear them too Nell?" Nell answered Dottie in a whisper, "You are quite correct Dottie, there are others here with us. This is their way of saying welcome to us, Dottie." Nell went on to explain, "the inhabitants of this realm originally did at one point in their long and distant past have bodies and forms like you and I, but they evolved. They moved beyond having to be physically seen, and developed such a sophisticated way of understanding each other, that they no longer had any use for their physical being. Their empathic nature evolved them into what they are now, they reveal themselves through sound only. But the one thing you can be sure of is, even if you cannot see anyone, you are never alone here." Nell continued, "they are all around us, they only want to greet you, and will do anything to help you, so pay attention now Dottie." At that very moment, a red flower with a yellow leaf was whizzing by; Dottie quickly grabbed it and squealed with delight,

"I caught it! I caught it, Nell."

"Oh, well done Dottie, very well done indeed. I hardly saw it myself, very good, now put it straight into your jar." All around them they could hear cheering and clapping. "We really must be on our way now, Dottie, as if we stay any longer, we will end up playing all day long. But we must keep focused, so come on now we best be going, you can come back here any time you like and play with them, but just not today, as we have important business to do," Nell said, giving Dottie a very serious look.

"Okay Nell, I understand, but I'll be back to play here as soon as I get my Cheromaack, so goodbye my invisible friends, goodbye to everyone in Mact, and thank you for the lovely flower," Dottie heard a collective murmur of farewell as they left through the orange-yellow door that suddenly reappeared before them.

CHAPTER 22

The Rainbow Flower

They were gathering speed now as they made their quest through the realms. "The next flower we must find is in the mysterious realm of *Welmaiyo*. Nell continued, although it's not actually a flower at first, it's a seed. We collect that little seed, and once it's placed into the jar, it grows instantly to become a fully grown plant in the mixture. It is called *The Rainbow Flower*: when you find a pod you need to crack it open and release its seed into the jar," Nell explained. As they approached the orange part of the rainbow, Nell instructed Dottie to knock three times on the door for it to open. "Here in the realm of Welmaiyo, it is always a lovely day. All the trees and plants have pods hanging from them ready to burst but there's never a single flower to be seen. Be warned Dottie, if you touch a tree or a plant then it divides and a brand-new plant forms instantly right next to it. The inhabitants, and any visitors here, must be very careful how they touch anything, so the place doesn't become too overgrown. Too much vegetation in here and then no one would be able to visit anymore. So, we have to tread really carefully and just pick the pod without touching the plant it hangs on," Nell warned. "So, it would be best if we use my Cheromaack to hover over the ground, here, hold on to me." Dottie looked down at the ground as they gently floated above it. When Dottie looked back, she could see the grass growing under where her feet had trodden and had left dark green grass footprints behind her. Nell and Dottie hovered above the grass and gently glided to where the seed pods were growing. Dottie leaned down and delicately picked one pod off its plant. She was careful to only touch the pod itself the whole time; opening it up to expose the shiny silver seed nestled inside. Dottie carefully placed the seed from the pod into her jar. Instantly, it started to grow in front of Dottie's eyes; first a stalk started to shoot up in the liquid, and then, as it reached the surface of the liquid, it budded. Next, each petal popped wide open, one at a time, all showing a different colour of the rainbow until all the petals were fully open. "Isn't it beautiful Dottie? I never tire of seeing The Rainbow Flower bloom, so wonderful," said Nell, a little lost in thought. "I will be taking you back here on a longer journey through this realm Dottie, they are all fascinating, but this one is truly exceptional, and I have yet to see all of it for myself, never had the time. But we will be coming back here again one day to explore its vast and unchartered territories. But for now – onward!"

CHAPTER 23

Mirror Images

I n the blink of an eye the duo arrived at the next entrance through the green part of the rainbow; the door was ornate and very tall. Dottie had to knock twice.

"I'm coming, I'm coming," she heard a familiar voice calling out from the other side of the door. As the door opened, a mirror image of Dottie appeared on the other side.

"It's me?!" Dottie was shocked by the sight of herself and looked questioningly at Nell. When she turned to look back this time, her lookalike was accompanied by a mirror image of Nell. Their doppelgängers spoke in unison, and both welcomed them to the realm of *Worltoc.*

"This is how the realm of Worltoc works Dottie, Nell said reassuringly. "No need to be concerned, the inhabitants of this realm adopt the physical appearances and behaviours of all who come here. Whoever visits this place is greeted by themselves, but it's just the way the folk who live here have adapted to visitors over hundreds and thousands of years. Now all of the occupants take on the image of whoever comes through the door." Nell continued, "at least we know who's in here with us at the moment, if there were others here then we would see carbon copies of them milling around the realm also." Suddenly, as Dottie looked around, she could see dozens more Dotties and Nells greeting them cheerily. Dottie was still in disbelief,

"Am I dreaming this Nell?"

"Not at all Dottie dear, everybody living in this realm will take on our image while we're visiting. I know it's a lot to take in, but you must understand, back in your realm you all adapted too. Humans never started out looking like you do now, you know, you were all quite hairy back in the early years, we wondered if you would ever progress past the hunter-gatherer stage, but eventually, with a little help from us, you did and hopefully for the better. Well, the same is true for the inhabitants of Worltoc, they have adapted in their own way," Nell said, trying to help Dottie make sense of it all.

"I think I understand, it's just there's so many mes and yous it's making me dizzy," she said while constantly looking all around her.

"You'll get very used to it the more you come back, I promise, but first, we must try to keep our minds on our task. Now, the next plant we are looking for is called *Blum*, it's a little plant that only grows on the ground under your feet, so if you lift up your foot, you'll discover this small little blue flower there." Sure enough, as soon as Dottie lifted her foot a little bunch of blue flowers were right there, and the moment Dottie picked just the one little flower the entire bunch disappeared. "If a flower is picked here it disappears from your sight until you next visit this realm where, once again, it will be waiting for you on the ground beneath your feet," Nell informed the little girl. "And once we leave here no one will look like us after we're gone, nothing will be disturbed and everything will be as it was, but nobody knows what that *was* is. Not one of my friends from the collective has ever glanced at the original inhabitants of Worltoc, and no one knows what they actually look like. There has never been a description or any documentation, drawing or otherwise of these inhabitants down through time," Nell explained.

"They are so mysterious," thought Dottie, and she vowed to come back and play with all the other Dotties and, perhaps she might even be lucky enough to be the first person to ever glance a Wortocian. But for now, that had to remain a wish for the future; Nell took her hand and, quick as a flash, they were on their way to the next realm.

CHAPTER 24

Dornia's Craft

Nell and Dottie landed at the yellow band of the rainbow.

"This is *Potenglashelm*, you will notice that the doorway itself is made from silica and very old glass. The lightest touch unlocks this door but only for those of the right character. But who are those with the right character you may ask? Only the door can decide. Everything here is made from silica and there is a yellow hue tinting the atmosphere, it's a place where you must do everything really gently and slowly, and not for very long. Now Dottie, this next plant known as, *Sanplat*, is similar to a plant growing in the sand dunes back in Blusfloct. It's a very hard plant to cut, so you have to use your magic scissors once again and be really delicate with it, until you're sure you have the entire plant cut before you place it in your jar." Dottie could see right through the door and to her it looked like everything was made of sand. She touched the door and it opened for her, she walked through really gently, then treaded very cautiously on the silica and glass like structures beneath her feet. "If you were to observe the structures under a microscope you would see how they resemble the pattern of snowflakes" Nell said, while carefully putting one foot in front of the other. "It may be wiser, once again, to hover over them, and that way avoid the ground altogether." So, she summoned her Cheromaack, and they both used it to glide the rest of the way just off the ground. The trees were also made out of silica;

everything was sandy and crystalline except for this little green plant jutting out, sporadically, from the sandy floor. It grew in little clusters around the whole area, so they went over to one such cluster. Dottie carefully knelt down first to survey the way the plant was situated, and then, gently started to place the scissors around it, so it would be cut at the right angle to cut it cleanly and intact. Then she carefully placed the entire long-stemmed plant into her jar.

"Good girl Dottie, very well done."

As they were departing from the realm of Potenglashelm, they were met by one of the realm-dwellers. A very grand and elegant lady stood before them who Nell introduced to Dottie. "Dottie, I would like you to meet Dornia, Keeper of the Crafts, and a very dear friend of mine. From time to time, we magic folk need a variety of tools of the trade. Dornia, and her fellow craft-masters, are the ones we rely on to provide us with the very best there is." Dornia spoke is a calm voice,

"I'm very honoured to meet this little one, as Virgil has been telling me how much Drackon warmed to her, I can see she has a pure heart, Nell." Then, touching Dottie's cheek she continued, "I wish you all the best in your ceremony today.

"Thank you very much Dornia," said Dottie, "Gosh, I love your coat."

"Thank you, I made it myself, and I'm so pleased you like it," Dornia said, giving her coat tails a little swish left and right. Dottie was barely listening as Nell and Dornia spoke. She was so entranced by Dornia's fashion, she noticed the wonderful long coat that the lady was wearing, and she was fascinated by the delicately embroidered flowers patterned all over it, in such exquisite detail, each petal seeming to change colour depending on which way it caught the light. Dornia's hair was a vibrant, shiny red colour piled upon her head, and held there with richly ornate hair combs and hairpins of silver and gold. Her face was dark and kindly, and she had a dazzling smile. Dornia handed Dottie a tiny little doll, perfect in every detail. Dottie was delighted with it and began to play. Nell and Dornia moved a little away from her and engaged in a very sombre conversation just out of earshot. Dottie was so busy playing with her new toy she didn't notice the time passing, and they had finished their discussion before she even noticed it had begun. Just before she left them, Dornia produced a crystal globe from under her coat and gave it to Nell. She held it up to the light, examining it in close detail. As Nell was holding this perfectly formed orb, Dottie noticed how it glowed with a light blue and green colour whenever Nell moved her hand over it. Nell was pleased.

"Thank you so much Dornia, this is wonderful work. I was so worried it was beyond repair, but it is flawless once again." Dornia closed her eyes for a moment and smiled in acknowledgement of Nell's thanks. "I had better do some crystal-gazing later on tonight before I consider what I must do next," Nell said. Dornia nodded seriously, then embraced Nell warmly and then Dottie, she wished them safe travels, then said her goodbyes to them both. As they made their way to the exit point from Potenglashelm, Nell explained, "only here can we get quality craft work that combines magic and skill. It is the master crafts people of Potenglashelm who make the best magic items, and these will help you with your work Dottie. They are our allies and comrades in the craft. Now, onto the next one," Nell commanded and off they went.

CHAPTER 25

The Goodness

A t the entrance to this realm Nell remarked, "We have only one more ingredient to gather before your ceremony.

"Oh, I'm so excited Nell, it's getting so close," exclaimed Dottie, so full of joy she was fit to burst. The last doorway of this quest was through the blue band of the rainbow. This doorway was made of very strong metal, ornately carved, and cast in a material similar in nature to bronze. "Oh, what a pretty doorway, Nell."

"This is one of the oldest doorways to one of the oldest realms and is guarded by a unicorn and a gatekeeper. Now remember, that the unicorn is the pinnacle of magical beings, so we must approach carefully, to give him time to accept you. Only then will he permit you to have the final ingredient," Nell advised. "Now dear, you only need to knock once, and the gatekeeper will open the door for us to enter." The gatekeeper was dazzlingly beautiful, and Dottie was amazed at her golden glow.

"Hello, we have been expecting you Dottie," she said, as she greeted Nell with a friendly nod and turned to the little girl. "There is only one being in this realm who can help you find your last ingredient Dottie, and once he makes up his mind, he will either give it over to you or not. This last part is based entirely on his decision about you," the gatekeeper explained.

The land laid out behind the doorway was very scenic, in fact, everything about the realm was scenic. There was a golden glow to it all, and the land seemed to stretch out far into the horizon. Everywhere one looked, there were graceful horses milling around and all about. Suddenly, there he was, she saw the white unicorn cantor up, and stand near the gatekeeper. He had a silken, flowing, mane and tail, and his coat was as shiny as diamonds in the sunshine. The unicorn's face was one of the prettiest faces Dottie had ever seen on a horse, or indeed, a unicorn for that matter.

"Hello there," she said gently to the unicorn, "you are the love-liest fellow I've ever seen." The unicorn, a naturally shy being, put his head down and scratched the ground with his shimmering hoof. He looked up at Dottie then slowly walked up to her. "Friends for life Dottie, he likes you," Nell noted with amazement, as she knew that usually he was slow to trust anybody. Dottie was mesmerized and put out her hand so the unicorn could nudge it. He put his head down near her, so she was able to stroke the side of his neck.

"Well now Dottie, I've never seen him take to anyone as quickly as you. Why you're a natural! Now you must walk by his side for a while so he can get to know you," the gatekeeper said.

Off the two of them went, while Nell stayed behind, this last test was something Dottie had to achieve on her own. Dottie was delighted, as she always wanted to meet a unicorn. Viola had said it was only a myth, but now she knew this to be un-true. Here Dottie was, walking side-by-side with a unicorn. Af-ter a while, they paused at a fence, and the unicorn bowed his head. Next, he knelt down on his front legs, giving a little snort, and somehow Dottie just knew that he was indicating that she should climb up on his back. He stood up fully again, and then with a happy whinny, he started to trot around in ever increasing circles. To her amazement, Dottie realised that the unicorn was starting to fly, and then they were airborne. Dottie could see all around her for miles and miles, she saw wonderful waterfalls, jungles, forests, and rolling hills with lush greenery as far as the eye could see. Suddenly, she felt the unicorn falter a little and wondered if something was wrong? Indeed, something was wrong, he could see a shadow in the distance that didn't belong there, darkness was descending over a patch of ground and growing larger and larger. There was no time to waste; the unicorn went into action and flew directly toward the shadow. He could not allow any badness to take hold in his realm, and knew this shadowy area was a dangerous manifestation. Right in the heart of the shadow a whirling witch was spinning round and around and seemed to be spreading the shadow ever wider. She flew up from the centre of the shadow and hovered directly in front of the unicorn and Dottie. All Dottie could do was watch in horror at the witch's behaviour. The closer the whirling witch got, the brighter the unicorn became; the growing intensity of the light emanating from him repulsing the snarling witch. Dottie felt totally safe in the unicorn's presence; even though the witch was growing larger and more fearsome. The witch squared up to him, looking directly at him, and had the most horrible eyes which were full of rage. Her eyes were blood red with large black pupils. Sensing she could not take much more of the unicorn's pure light, she had thoughts of grabbing hold of Dottie and taking her back to her bad realm. Dottie was unafraid as she could feel the unicorn's pure energy protecting her. The witch was spinning like a top and screaming at the unicorn. She might have thought she was fearsome, but all Dottie could think was how much she reminded her of Viola in one of her rages.

The unicorn was calm, and steadfast in dealing with this witch from the realm of Sherastnorth. It was Sherida, she had come back after a long absence, and she was having notions of taking over his realm. Sherida thought that this time she had

developed the ultimate new potion using the Greana that her
Trinics had gathered for her back in Vilshoct. Her Greana potion gave her the power to control shadows and she planned to
use that power to engulf the Goodness's realm in darkness,
and ultimately, to cover The Goodness with a thick shadow
and thereby shield herself from his light. With it, she had
thought to overpower the unicorn for once and for all, but she
was wrong; his power only seemed to increase in her presence.
Dottie had to avert her eyes as the light was so bright emanating from him, and she could feel a great sense of protection
from it, something she did not fully understand at all, but she
was cocooned by it and was only an observer of this meeting
between good and bad. He started to glow brighter and
brighter and Sherida recoiled from it, her anger being absorbed
within this light, he had her suspended in it. Dottie got a good
look at her before she had to shut her eyes tight. Sherida
started to shrink in size, smaller and smaller, and in less than a
minute Sherida was but a speck of dust being blown out of the
realm and back to where she came from. She was always trying
his patience and sometimes she would take quite a bit of a bat-
tering before she would retreat. This time was no different; he
had shone brighter to shrink her down temporarily and his
pure, cleansing, light also purged the maliciousness from her
being. This had now rendered her harmless for many months.
Once back in her own realm of Sherastnorth, she would rapidly return to her normal size. A very disorientated Sherida
would run a stall at the local market, selling cheap trinkets and
badly knitted hats under her alternate name of Volti, until her
bad powers were restored once more. There was one thing no
bad entity could handle, and that was the pure light of The
Goodness; but they never seemed to learn.
Dottie waited till he was back on the ground, when it was truly
over, and he had completed his task, she patted him on the
neck, and he gently knelt so she could climb down. He shook

his great mane and made a breathing noise nudging her a few times. She could sense that he was telling her she was truly brave in the face of such a threat. He knew she was more than ready to receive the final ingredient and he led her into a vast field full of flowers, he took his time as he slowly walked through the field with Dottie to locate the last magical ingredient growing in this realm, thus enabling her to complete her quest. Once he located where this elusive flower was, he plucked it carefully, then he turned his head to Dottie and gently placed this magical flower the *Azr*, a delicate bloom of light pink into her little hand. She gazed at this pretty little pink flower, her favourite colour, and placed it in her jar. She was mesmerised as the unicorn looked into her eyes, any trauma from their previous encounter melted away, he made a little breathing sound and nudged Dottie giggling as she patted him. They walked along for a while, and she rubbed his neck a few more times, she really couldn't quite believe how happy she felt and what a spectacular event she'd just witnessed.

"So that was one of the bad rulers of Sherastnorth," she thought to herself, and could see the unicorn nod his head, neighing in confirmation. Despite the earlier trauma, she thought that this fabulous place was just her cup of tea, as she patted his neck, he snorted and raised his head up and down gently understanding everything. She felt like she never wanted to leave as they both walked back to where Nell was waiting. Nell greeted Dottie as she arrived back.

"I see you met Sherida, she is always trying to come in and take over, every time she tries, it sets her back for years, she never gives up and she will be back. We are just so used to it now and it always cheers us up as we get a dose of his great light. Now that you have experienced bathing in his light too dear, you have been given a new strength from it. We too have felt the effects of it," Nell said. Dottie noticed how youthful Nell looked and was glowing a little like the gatekeeper.

The gatekeeper had set up a special tea party to celebrate Dottie's gathering of all the ingredients for her first official magic potion and congratulated the little girl on her great bravery in facing the terrible Sherida. She had prepared a lovely picnic for them all, full of treats and delicious cakes and even some sweet parsnips for the beautiful unicorn. She had a great display laid out on a large table; the finest elegant porcelain tableware was placed on the crisp linen tablecloth much to Dottie's delight. "Tea should never be rushed, the gatekeeper said. Even when there's no time; there's always time for tea!" Nell and Dottie clapped their hands with delight, and in chorus responded, "Here! Here!" They took their seats; she then served the tea, and they listened as Dottie recounted her version of all that had occurred in her own inimitable way.

After a time, and after countless cups of refreshing tea, plenty of tasty sandwiches, and delicious cakes, they had to say their farewells. Dottie put her face up to the side of the great unicorn's downward stretched head, wishing she never, ever, had to leave him. He nudged her gently and Dottie felt very emotional at their parting. Nell took her hand.

"Come along now child, we must be going." They both said their goodbyes to the gatekeeper and to the unicorn.

"Oh, I wish I didn't have to leave him, Nell, he's so beautiful, isn't he?" Dottie exclaimed with tears in her eyes.

"Yes, a most precious friend, we all treasure him greatly, there are no words to describe how great he is, and how much he does to protect us all. This is why we have named him simply, 'The Goodness,'" Nell said, with tears of emotion welling-up in her eyes too simply at the thought of him.

"Ahem," she cleared her throat, "well – ahem, you know you can visit him anytime you feel like it, once you have your very own Cheromaack, so come along now." Of course, on hearing this, Dottie cheered up no end, she felt happier to leave now, knowing she could plan her return.

The Graduand

They were now nearing their goal. "We must be getting on our way to the indigo doorway," Nell exclaimed. She was excited at the prospect of her young charge being indoctrinated into the great collective of magic. Dottie would then take her place alongside Nell and the many great sorcerers from all the other realms. "Once the jar is complete it should become a clear blue sparkling liquid and then it is ready to consume."

"Oh, I'm so excited Nell, I feel I have made so many new friends in all these beautiful places, I can't wait for my ceremony."

"I'm so happy that this great day has come at last, Dottie my dear."

Just as they approached the doorway of the indigo band, it flew open of its own accord, in anticipation of their arrival. On the other side of the doorway, a red carpet of flowers was growing right under their feet. It stretched out ahead of them all the way up to the Hill of Farne itself. When they reached the hill, they were greeted by a vast gathering, an endless array of folk, all different shapes, and sizes, from all corners of all the realms. All were waiting there to witness a momentous occasion, Dottie's graduation.

"Nell, have they all showed up just for me?" Dottie whispered with shock and great surprise.

"But of course they have Dottie, they encourage all new young protégés like you, everyone is so happy for you, and only want to wish you well. Once you complete your ceremony, all here know that the more support you gain from The Collective; the more successful you will become. This benefits all, and all wish you the best start in this magical pursuit. Believe me, this is of great importance to us all Dottie," Nell said, in all seriousness. "Oh, I hope I don't let anyone down," Dottie said, looking every one of her seven-and-a-half years.

"Don't worry my dear, you can't let anybody down, they're all here to support you, just as once they all supported me, and all the others who went before. Power comes from within, from believing in yourself, it is true, but power also comes from without, through the belief others have in you, and when those combine, you become unstoppable," she exclaimed, trying to put Dottie's mind at ease. Dottie felt very happy after hearing those reassuring words from Nell. "Just enjoy this time now, you've already earned it Dottie, this is the fun bit."

"Fun! Fun is FUN," she thought, and Nell laughed. At that moment, the head of the C.O.R., The Grandmaster Sorcerer, appeared and welcomed Nell warmly with a great smile and bowed. Nell turned and motioned for her young charge to step forward and then introduced Dottie to him. He was a very old man with a long, long beard and a head of thick white hair, he also appeared to have a golden glow about him and a wonderful smile, Dottie warmed to him immediately returning a bright smile.

"Very pleased to meet you, sir."

Oh, my dear, what a pleasure it is to finally meet you too, we are all so happy that you've decided to take the time to carry on the magic tradition with us. You're such a great ambassador for us all. Everyone who has met you can't stop speaking highly enough about you.

Oh, thank you sir. You are very kind. My goodness, you've such a lovely white beard," Dottie observed.

"Why thank you my dear, I grew it myself you know," said Herb, and Dottie laughed. "My name is Herb," he said, "erm, because….er, because it's my name!" then he chuckled and talked to himself.

"Herb, it's an honour to meet you," said Dottie performing a small curtsey.

"The honour is all yours, I'm sure, yes, yes, indeed," replied Herb with a giggle and shaking her hand vigorously.

"Oh Herb," said Nell, with a wry smile.

"Now my child, if and when you're ready, we shall begin. Nell, would you be so kind as to initiate this new candidate?" Nell nodded silently, closed her eyes for a few moments, her hands, down by her sides, then turned slowly, and she raised them, bringing her hands, palms turned inwards, a little away from her face. Although her lips did not appear to move, her soft incantation could be clearly heard by all present. The liquid in Dottie's jar now began to swirl and fizz, and turned a speckled shade of translucent blue, it sparkled throughout with a golden shimmer. Nell slowly opened her eyes, their colour seemed to have intensified, and she nodded to Dottie, it was time. They had practiced the procedure in the days leading up to this ceremony several times, so that Dottie would remember how to do it correctly. She raised her jar up to the sky, then making sure that she was standing on top dead centre of the Hill of Farne, she drank the sparkling liquid brew, holding it in her left hand, as they had practiced. She did not hesitate, but drank it all back in one go, she noticed the taste was like marshmallows, vanilla with honeysuckle, and such great sweetness, she was sorry when it was all gone. She licked the inside of the jar until the last drop was drained. Dottie looked to Nell, then looked out over the myriad folk assembled to witness her ceremony. Their excited chatter quieted, and silence fell over the entire place, even the birdsong had paused. Suddenly, a whooshing sound came over the horizon, everyone looked up to try and see it, a shape streaked overhead, turning, and swooping like an eagle, its downwash was felt as it skimmed just above the heads of all those gathered there. Then, it stopped, hovered for a moment, and slowly but gently made its way right to the top of the Hill of Farne. First it brushed around Herb, tickling his beard, and causing him to giggle, then it paused in front of Nell, and to Dottie's mind, it appeared to bow respectfully before it turned and sought out Dottie. It had a wonderful calming aura about it. Slowly and softly, it wrapped itself around Dottie until it had covered her entirely, momentarily she was encased in it, but she didn't feel afraid. Instead, she felt warm and protected by it, as it wrapped itself around her; she felt a kinship to it in a way she would never be able to describe. It was so soft to the touch, yet immeasurably strong, and it had a wonderfully rich aroma, which Dottie inhaled fully, while its material had a shimmering hint of a purple sheen to it. The Cheromaack unwrapped itself and was now draped over Dottie's little shoulders like a cape. Dottie felt herself being lifted up by it and suddenly she was flying through the air, she chuckled with delight as she soared high above the clouds. At first, the Cheromaack was in control, but instinctively Dottie began to take over, gliding first to the left, then right, getting a feel for it. There was a symbiosis between her and the Cheromaack, and it would take back control whenever Dottie's enthusiasm got the better of her, and before she got herself into any danger. If ever she felt unsure, it seemed the cloak could sense this and corrected any misjudgement of speed or attitude. She grew and grew in her ability and soon she was performing loop-the-loops and daring reverse dives.

"This is so amazing," she thought, as all the clouds were whooshing by and the colours of the land below flickering past at lightning speed, so fast she felt she could fly to the moon and back in a flash. When Dottie started to think of it going at a slower pace, it slowed down. Dottie was a quick learner and was now in full control, and with one last flourish she cork-screwed up high into the clouds, then slowly descended back down to land on the top of the Hill of Farne, once more, to great applause. Having completed her maiden flight, and sworn an oath, Dottie was now part of the magic collective in the Council of Realms. Dottie felt very honoured, justly proud, and very pleased with herself indeed. The Cheromaack gently rose from her shoulders and whizzed off into the far distance, but Dottie knew it would always be there at a moment's notice if needs be. Once she was back amongst the congregation, Nell and Herb were applauding and everyone was cheering for her. A great party ensued, and all celebrated in her honour. There were flowers strewn everywhere, tables with every con-fectionary one could wish for, overhead there was a big banner with the words:

"Well done, Dottie!" Everyone was cheering and laughing, and in high spirits as they waited for Dottie to take her place at the head of the great table. There were games and music and songs being sung in celebration, Nell sat next to her on one side, and Herb sat on the other.

"This is all for me?" she asked, in amazement.

"Of course, we are celebrating your great success, and this is your day my dear, so enjoy it all for today we celebrate YOU!" Nell said, laughing. Then, she picked up a glass of fizzy pink liquid, held it up in her hand bringing all to a respectful, if giddy, silence. Everyone raised a glass to toast Dottie and a cheer rose up once more,

"Three cheers for Dottie Moorehead - hip hip hooray! Hip Hip hooray! HIP HIP HOORAY!" A spontaneous standing ovation broke out as flower petals floated down over her from above. Later after the party had ended, and as she had promised, Nell had Dottie home just in time for tea, magically, although Dottie had eaten so much cake, and drank so much lemonade, she did not feel in the least bit full.

"What a great day," Dottie said, as she hugged Nell.

"What a great day indeed," replied Nell. "Now go child, go be with your family, and enjoy your family tea. Nell bid her a good evening and with a whoosh she was gone.

CHAPTER 27

The Little Aviator

Dottie had learned, from bitter experience, that sharing her happiness with her elder sister was the surest way of ending it, so, this time, she was not going to tell anyone about her magical adventures. Viola gave her some strange looks wondering what was wrong with her.

"What are you giggling about, Dottie, come on, share the joke?" Viola snapped. She was sure that Dottie was up to something and was sick of her always looking like the cat that got the cream. Dottie knew from all their previous interactions that there was no need to tell her sister the truth. She did not even believe it when Dottie told her she had seen that brown fox at the gate, so she would never believe the magical adventures that Dottie was having, there was no point in telling her. Dottie concocted a plausible reason for her jocularity,

"I was just thinking about the funny cat I saw today, he was just so friendly, so I ended up playing with him all afternoon."

"Stay well away from those old wild cats, Dottie, her grandmother mumbled, "filthy auld things, always at my bins," leaving the room muttering to herself.

Dottie went to bed early that evening, dreaming of the most amazing day that she just had, and was quite sure every day, from then on in, would never be quite the same again. No longer did she feel the need to seek her sister's approval since all the sorcerers thought of her as worthy of their respect. She felt she could achieve anything she set her mind to now. She loved her family, and she never wanted to be a worry to them, as they would never understand all the exciting things she got up to now as a junior sorcerer. Her family were glad that Dottie no longer seemed to get into any mischief, not realising how many adventures she was having in the many realms of the rainbow. From that momentous day onwards, Dottie's Cheromaack was her guardian. She would practice calling it and it would be there in an instant, no matter the time, no matter the weather. She was so eager for her next adventure to begin, but until then, Nell had told her she had to just practice and bide her time. Each day she could not wait to summon her Cheromaack to go training with it; she would scoff down her breakfast, dash out through the kitchen door, and up to a clearing in the woods. She would close her eyes, imagine herself soaring upwards, and as soon as she had that thought, she would hear that now familiar whooshing sound. Her Cheromaack would land on her shoulders and then she would be up and away. She soared as high as an eagle and her mornings were spent joyfully practising her flying skills with this wondrous magical entity. After a few hours of training, while on her lunch break, one afternoon, she daydreamed of how she might one day start a competition for all the new recruits. A game to test their aerial skills; it would help with practicing their flying until they would all become experts in the use of their Cheromaacks. It would be ground-breaking in the magical world she thought. She could start a magical Olympic games between all the recruits from the other realms. Through sporting competition, they would all improve as aviators. After a lovely lunch of egg and cress sandwiches, and a flask of hot tea, Dottie dozed off dreaming such dreams.

CHAPTER 28

A Friend in Need

After several weeks had passed, one morning when Dottie visited Nell's house, she called-out her name as she usually did before walking through the, forever-open, kitchen door. Nell was sitting at the table, lost in thought, with a very concerned look on her face.

"Hello Dottie, how are you today?"

"I'm ok, but why do you look so sad?" Dottie asked.

"It's just an old friend of mine has gotten herself into a spot of bother, it's nothing to worry about, I'm sure. In fact, myself and another old friend of mine, a wonderful lady called Juni, are going to check on her. I'm sure everything will be fine," Nell said. "So, while I'm away, do keep up your studies, feed the cat, and make sure the weeds don't overrun the vegetable patch." What Nell was not telling her young friend, was that there were serious issues with one sorcerer in particular, an old friend of Nell's called, Mai. After she had her crystal orb repaired by Dornia in Potenglashelm, she had been viewing Mai's activities and the goings-on in Sherastnorth. Nell had consulted with the wise elders and was thinking of how best to resolve the situation for The Collective. Nell and Juni explained to them, "Mai seems to have gotten herself into a rather sticky spot in that realm. We're both deeply concerned for her safety, and appeal to The Collective to permit us to venture in there and execute a rendition. I fear it will be risky, and we shall have to leave you all for a while, until myself and Juni can sort it all out. It's not a task that we look forward to at all, I can tell you, because we either return with Mai; or not at all." Having considered Nell and Juni's request, The C.O.R. all agreed that they were the ones best suited for this onerous task. Back in Nell's kitchen, a tearful Dottie was heard to say,

"What – I have to stay here, why can't I go with you? Oh, please, can I come with you? Maybe I can help in some way?" pleaded Dottie.

"No, my dear, not this time, I'm afraid you're not quite ready, it requires very experienced magic knowledge indeed, which I fear you do not yet possess."

"Oh, but Nell, I can learn as I go along, I'm a fast learner, please, please let me go with you," Dottie entreated. Sensing that Dottie was getting close to tears, the old tutor realised she owed the child a further explanation.

"Dottie dear, listen to me carefully, you see, many years ago, a good friend of mine called Mai, one of our greatest sorcerers, became corrupted and rejected the C.O.R. In the beginning, she had shown tremendous promise; she was so good and a kindly being to all, but at some point, along the way something happened to her, she changed. We had thought, with a little encouragement, she could be brought back on course, that was until we learnt that recently she decided to move to Sherastnorth and live there permanently. The bad magic in that realm is powerful, and has a strong hold over her, so much so, it has her mesmerized, and now she has been nothing but trouble ever since. We've tried to help her numerous times, and show her the error of her ways, but she thinks she knows what's best for her, and no longer listens to any one of us. She's gotten so caught up and entangled with the bad energies of Sherastnorth that it's completely brainwashed her. She does nothing but bad things now, and she has turned her back on our good magic ways. By her using her magic in Sherastnorth, she doesn't realise its negative energy is steadily draining her, she thinks it's making her stronger. She's gradually losing herself with each passing day, and every time she casts a bad spell, we lose another little bit of our old friend Mai. The same thing would happen to you or me Dottie, if we are out of the good light for too long it can dim it and the badness can overpower any sorcerer, no matter how powerful they might be. It drags them downwards into the darkness without them even being aware of it. It is, of course, also a choice you make, and if a sorcerer believes in the good magic, and stays true, then it becomes stronger. But, with bad magic, using it can eat away at your spirit. It convinces you that its badness is stronger than good, and on a rare occasion, if you weaken at all with doubt, it can penetrate deeper into your subconscious, this is what happened to Mai many years ago. With the right guidance you can stay strong against it, but you have to always be aware of it, and you have to be battle-ready at all times against it, so as not to get drawn into doing its bidding." Nell explained it all as clearly as she could, she wanted to inform her student and impress on the attentive little girl the gravity of her mission. Dottie nodded, taking in every word. For a moment, Dottie joked with herself in her head; she thought Viola must have ventured in there at some point, which would explain her mean behaviour. "This is no laughing matter and shouldn't be taken lightly," Nell scolded telepathically. It is a very dangerous place if you're not strong or prepared for it, then you will be overwhelmed my child. I promise I will prepare you for it as best I can because you will have to go there some day when you're older. It is the ultimate test of your magic powers, we have all gone through it, and I'm afraid my old friend Mai, has gotten sucked in and succumbed to the place's bad energies."

"I see, ok then, I guess I understand why I can't go with you this time." Dottie reluctantly agreed to her old mentor's reasoning as to why it would be unwise for her to go with her on this occasion.

"Here, I've pulled out my oldest book on magic for you, which I've left on the kitchen table. If you read a chapter a day, and practice the spells, you will get a good basic understanding of what we do. By the time I return, have it read from cover-to-cover for me," she directed.

"I'll have it learnt off by heart Nell, this is the kind of home-work that I love – magic homework," said Dottie, brightening a little.

Once Nell was sure her student was feeling better about her leaving, she went to her back room; opened a large chest of drawers and selected certain vials and charms that she felt might be needed for the task ahead. Presently, Nell bid a fond farewell to little Dottie, then summoned her Cheromaack, turned and smiled at the little girl. Then Nell looked skyward, and with a loud *whoosh* she was up high into the clouds and gone.

Booksmart with Tresseld

As the days turned into weeks, Dottie, who was, after all, still only a very young child, soon wearied of the daily routine. She had tried her best to be a diligent scholar but found herself easily distracted. There was always something far more interesting happening outside, in Nell's cottage garden, than being stuck indoors practicing and reading dusty old spell books. She watched as ants carried large twigs along in rows and back down into their nests. She marvelled at the little Hummingbird Moth who came each day to drink nectar from Nell's lavender plants. Soon, she had abandoned even the basic daily chores Nell had set for her, and the floors remained un-scrubbed, and the windows unwashed, she was, after all, a little girl.

It wasn't until one sunny afternoon in late spring, just before the changing of the season, when Dottie had busied herself setting up a game of hopscotch outside the cottage; lining the paving slabs with chalk numbers and using an old shoe polish tin as her marker. She had begun to play, and in the way that children usually do, she became engrossed in her game, so engrossed in fact that she barely noticed the sound of someone clearing their throat as if trying to catch Dottie's attention. "Hallo – Hallo there…" came the voice from within Nell's kitchen. "Hallooo – can you not hear me girl?" came the rather stern voice.

Dottie was busy playing hopscotch and trying to keep count of how many hops she had taken. She had decided to compete against an imaginary version of Viola – and right now, she seriously suspected Viola was cheating.

"Oh, this is intolerable,' came the voice from the kitchen 'Halloo there young miss…. can I have a wee word with ye? Hallooo…HALLOOOO!"

Suddenly from the kitchen there was an almighty thud, followed by some unintelligible Gaelic swear words – THAT caught young Dottie's attention. She walked gingerly toward the kitchen door…….

"Is… is there anybody there?" she asked sheepishly.

"DOWN here – down HERE," said a rather muffled voice.

To Dottie's amazement, the voice appeared to be coming from the rather large book of spells that seemed to have fallen from its lectern and onto the kitchen floorboards all by itself. Dottie carefully picked the heavy book up by its cover and replaced it back onto the lectern.

"Are….are you okay?" enquired a puzzled Dottie.

"Yes, yes, yes, child I'm perfectly fine, my bindings are of the highest quality, and a fall or two will not take a whip out of me, I can assure ye. I'm Tresseld by the way…. Your appointed tutor in all things spectacular and magical…. But I've been waiting now for an age and a half for you to bother taking the slightest bit of an interest in your studies. Ye seem far more concerned in leppin' about like a frog with an itch, than tending to yer studies, me lassie," said the book in an authoritarian voice that seemed to be just short of shouting. Dottie blushed a little,

"I'm sorry Mr Tresseld I…"

"Let me stop you there me lass. I'm not in the slightest bit interested in yer excuses or yer explanations," interrupted the book, "Ye have wasted weeks already and the sooner ye knuckle down to some reading and study the better."

Rightly chastened, Dottie went straight to work, pulling a chair back from the table, with an intake and then an outtake of breath she placed a different big heavy book on it, then a pretty pink cushion on top of that, so she would be at the right height, and all set up and comfortable. She took her time climbing up onto the chair but as soon as she was settled, she took another outtake of breath, fixed her hair, and then began to read this great tome. However, when she was about to open the cover and read the first page, she found that the book forced its covers closed and, struggle as she might to open it, she could not. She wondered if she was imagining it all and once again attempted to open the cover.

"Not so fast ye wee young scamp. Who are ye to be opening my pages, pages that contain knowledge and wisdom set down by scribes from a time beyond time? This knowledge is power, this knowledge is priceless, this is no instruction manual, THIS is no cookbook. There are protocols to be observed, procedures to be followed. Ye must announce yerself first, and request that I will grant ye access to me pages, that ye might set yer eyes on the wisdom of the eons."

After the initial shock of never having seen a book behave in such a fashion before, Dottie just stared at it for a while, and realised that everything about learning magic was magic also.

"Please, I beg your pardon, Mr. Tresseld," she responded nervously.

"I'm nay a Mr nor a Mrs, a Miss nor a Master, a King nor a Queen, I'm no Senator nor a Doctor, I'm nay a Sage nor a Seer, I'm all of these and none, I am Tresseld, if ye must address me, I would prefer it if ye just called me Tresseld, that's title enough for me," he said crossly, still resentful at her for ignoring him for so long.

"You know I think that's a lovely name, Tresseld, may I call you Tress for short?" Dottie asked with a hopeful smile.

"No, ye may certainly not Missy, you will call me Tresseld if you're to call me anything at all," he responded quite firmly. "I'm awfully sorry Tress-held…. oh, please don't be offended, Tresseld it is." Dottie took a deep breath and announced herself to the book. "My name is Dottie Moorehead, I am seven and a half years old. I'm a very good friend of Nell's and she usually teaches me all kinds of interesting things, but she had to head off in an awful hurry on important magic business, so she asked me to read you from start to finish, and I promised her I would have learned you off by heart by the time she returns."

"Ok, that's a bit better," the book replied, "but I very much doubt that, as I'm a very complex book to learn off by heart in a short space of time. Ye have already delayed with all yer tomfoolery, I guard all the spells in me and some of them are a lot to remember for a wee girly such as the likes of ye," he said smugly.

"Well, you must let me try then to prove you wrong?" Dottie said, instantly detecting a challenge ahead for her to overcome. "I'm game if ye are Dottie, now ye may open me up and stop at the very first page."

Dottie was fascinated with what she saw; inside the book was laid out with beautiful handwriting, in black ink decorated with gold flowers, the more she read the more beautiful the book seemed to become. Nell had often noted to Dottie that books respond to their readers, and also, deteriorate with neglect. The dark brown cover, which initially seemed like old worn and cracked leather, had transformed. Now, its cover binding was of the most beautiful soft leather, and gold embossed animals and plants intertwined, these would come alive and move freely all over it under the reader's gaze. The edges of the cover were encased in a golden metal frame and in the centre was a lockable hasp. Currently it was unlocked, as Nell had used a magic key to open it before she left. The first page was filled with written instructions and illustrations on how to concoct the first spell. When Dottie began to read the spell aloud, the illustrations came to life and became three-dimensional characters acting out a spell, so the reader could see what was being described in the text. Dottie was flabbergasted and thrilled simultaneously.

"Why can't they teach us like this at school?" she asked, "this is such fun!" She would soon learn that Tresseld's terse nature was that of an excellent tutor, and one who was enthused by his subject matter, and excited to pass on even the smallest part of his vast knowledge to a willing and diligent student. Dottie was careful not to rile him though, and from then on, when it came to study time, she was alert and keen as mustard. Tresseld warmed to his new student quickly, he may have been a curmudgeon at times, but he was always an excellent tutor. He explained to Dottie, in precise detail, what she was reading, and that he would be her guide through the entire book. He had informed her that studies began at:

"08.30 hours, sharp, no excuses accepted," and she needed to be in Nell's kitchen each morning, Saturdays included.

Dottie did not mind one little bit, as this was the kind of teacher she would have loved at school. No matter how many questions Dottie had, Tresseld was able to second guess them. He knew from reading Dottie's mind what she was unsure of and was able to explain it again and again to Dottie till she understood it completely.

"There are no bad students," he would always proclaim, "Only bad teachers!" His methodology was straightforward, it required patience and persistence. "Once a child understands something, Dottie, they never forget it, it's only when they pretend to understand something that they get truly lost. Never be afraid to ask questions, again and again and again. It is the only way to learn. Once you truly comprehend, only then will you have learned. Understand all that is written on my pages, then ye shall excel in everything magical into yer future and get the best out of yer Cheromaack," he said with a quiet confidence that reassured Dottie. "I know it might seem like a lot to take in at times, it was the same for Nell when she was learning these exact same spells ye're undertaking now. Nell and I can still recall how she too could feel a bit intimidated by having to learn so much."

"You knew Nell when she was a child, Tresseld?" Dottie asked in a surprised tone.

"But of course, I did, where do ye think she gets all her wisdom from?" he said, with no small amount of pride. "I have passed through the hands of all the greatest practitioners since – well since long before I care to mention," said the book. Dottie began her study with Tresseld in earnest, learning the first spell of the book with aplomb; she presented every morning at 8:30 am on the dot, she worked hard, but of course making her mistakes too.

"Mistakes are just learning the way not to do something," Tresseld would reassure her. "It is nay an easy task to turn a mouse into a cat!" She would start out fine but then turning mice into half mouse, half cat, was surprisingly entertaining, as it kept trying to chase itself. Dottie would follow the instructions again and again but somehow would always forget some small little detail, which was obviously always vital to a spell, and she had to remember to include everything. "There are no shortcuts," Tresseld would reiterate. So, she learnt by trial and error, as she had obviously missed something minute, but very important and set it to rights. Then she was able to turn the mice into fully fledged cats and then turn them back to mice again which she repeated until she had it completely learnt off by heart. Tresseld gave a big cheer, "Well done me girl, ye've cracked it!" he shouted out with great relief sometimes clapping his cover together by way of applauding his little student's success. While no animals were ever harmed in any way when conducting this spell, in fact, they had no memory of it at all, so carried on as normal once back in their original body. However, the cats gained a healthy respect for mice after that spell, and would tend to let the mice scurry by, back into their mouse holes rather than chase them for sport. Once Dottie had the first spell under her belt, she began to really make progress, she made sure that she left nothing out, no matter how trivial, and was now building up a respectable repertoire of helpful little spells, that she could recreate at the drop of a hat. These were the foundations in magic upon which she would build. "If ye don't learn your ABCs, then ye'll never know your XYZs," Tresseld would say again and again. He had a distinct turn of phrase when it came to sayings and liked to play with clichés, "Rome wasn't built in a day," he would declare but then add "… but it *could* have been with magic," then he would chuckle to himself. For every saying Tresseld made, he would always add a magic solution. She enjoyed every moment learning all about Tresseld too, and how he was always a book. He was originally self-published but created a whole publishing house with many other publications and revised editions, as he was very popular when he came into being. He was there at the start of magic, after all he was a first edition. He kept adding pages to himself with each new spell or potion, once discovered, each new spell was then developed and refined. There was nothing he did not know, as he was always on trend, which he was immensely proud of. When Dottie would compliment him on his great knowledge, you could see his pages puff up with pride.

Tresseld was very impressed by his young student's rapid progress,

"Dottie every day ye've been here on time and ye've understood all the spells with alacrity, I must say. I'm very impressed with yer advancement," he said proudly.

"Thank you," said Dottie, not quite sure of the meaning of all Tresseld's words, but appreciating that he was praising her, "it's easy when I've such a great teacher." Tresseld, despite his protestations to the contrary, was not averse to a well-placed compliment or two.

"Aye true enough, true enough." Her praise was merited and elicited a pleasant surprise for the little girl when Tresseld came to a decision, "Dottie, do ye know something?" he said, "I think yer studiousness deserves its own reward and it's my belief that ye're quite ready for one of the more powerful of spells, the gift of telepathy; the ability of reading the thoughts of others."

"Well about time too Tresseld," Dottie responded with a cheeky smile.

"Hmmph!" he remarked back, never quite sure how to take her gentle mocking of his fustiness, and went on,

"Yes…well…quite…however, I had to make sure ye were ready for this gift, as it can be a little difficult at first to switch off ye know. Ye really, really, don't want to hear what yer mother, father, sister, or even yer grandmother for that matter, is thinking about, that's for sure. Believe you me, me girl!" he said rather uncomfortably, as if recalling some past disagreeable memory of his own.

"I know," said Dottie, unsure that her delicate young mind would ever fully recover from such an incident. "But if Nell has the ability to tune out, then that's something I'm sure I want to learn too, once I've mastered it, I'll be able to completely ignore my family's thoughts, and my sister's thoughts. Yuck… can you imagine hearing HER thoughts, if she has any?!" she paused, thought for a moment then with a shudder said even louder, "Ugh!" Giving it a bit more consideration, Dottie added, "In a way I guess it's a little bit like the ringing I sometimes get in my ears, if I think about it then it gets louder, but when I focus on the farthest away sound, the leaves rustling in a breeze, a blackbird singing, the waves breaking on the shore, then the ringing just goes away," nodding to herself as she was considering her idea.

"Well now," said Tresseld, "that is indeed a very good way of putting it Dottie, that's exactly how ye control this power, there would be just too much noise all at once if ye didn't know how to filter out all that chatter ye see." Tresseld was pleased at how his student had instinctively come up with a solution all on her own, he continued to be surprised at Dottie's natural ability to learn and adapt so well, a reflection on his own expert tuition no doubt, he thought. "This is a spell where ye'll need to use yer Cheromaack, so just imagine it in yer mind and visualise it making its way to ye and it will be here. In fact, to achieve this spell, well, actually, for many of the more advanced spells, ye'll need yer Cheromaack. Ye have only just been recently inaugurated, so ye must tread carefully with it while it learns to trust ye fully, and until ye've full use of all its magical powers. These will grow and grow the more ye use it, in fact, some say they find out new abilities their Cheromaacks possess every time they use it, even those who have had their Cheromaack, for years and years. Although, it might be easy to disregard them as just a mere tool to be used in the magical arts, I suspect we have never fully harnessed their true potential," mused Tresseld, now lost in his own thoughts, flapping a few dog-eared pages back and forth. There followed a long, awkward silence, which Dottie knew meant Tresseld was postulating and theorising in his mind, and probably adding a new appendix to his chapter on the Cheromaack. She knew it was best not to interrupt and have him lose his train of thought. Presently, Tresseld emerged from his trance-like state.

"Anyway, now, where was I? Oh yes, the telepathy, to begin… here girl, the instructions are here for ye to read for yerself on me pages," opening himself up at the correct page. Dottie read this aloud.

"The candidate must go to the realm of Sherastsouth in the blue band of the rainbow and seek The Goodness's permission to visit *The Crystal Mountain* in his realm, if given, he will then grant you the right to hold the sacred white crystal chalice that is kept there in *The Cave of Magical Light*. Once inside, it will only light up if it will allow you to begin. If you are passed by the light, then you will be able to speak your spell aloud, written below, the light will then bathe you, and it will bestow onto you the gift of telepathy. As part of the process, the candidate must use the chalice to gather the water from, *The Pool of Illumination*, to seat the gift within themselves, otherwise, the ability will be fleeting and will fade over time."

"I want ye to have all the information and instruction in front of ye on me pages, ye must look and learn it all off by heart. It must all be performed exactly as described here in. Once ye're ready, and have committed it all to heart, then ye just think of yer Cheromaack and it will come to ye," Tresseld remarked. "No matter where ye are, it'll find ye and fly ye to wherever yer going."

"You've reminded me about this now more than once before, Mr. repeaty-pants," said Dottie cheekily. Tresseld however was very indignant by his young charge's insolence.

"I was ONLY trying to help ye…ye impertinent little girl. Ye're too impetuous and that can be a danger, what ye need to learn now is some patience," Tresseld snapped his cover huffily, and locked his hasp and staple, then made both disappear, so no matter how much Dottie tried to open his cover, it was just impossible. She realised, that for a hard-covered book, Tresseld could be very thin-skinned.

"I'm sorry, Tresseld, please come back, I didn't mean to insult you, pretty please," she begged, albeit a little bit cheekily. She spent the next few hours tidying up the kitchen and dusting down Tresseld's cover, even giving his wooden plinth a once-over with some lavender and beeswax polish which she knew was his favourite.

Eventually, as the afternoon drifted by, he slowly shifted and reopened his cover and composed himself once more. The lesson continued to its end without any further incident, and Dottie focused on her work diligently, showing proper respect towards the work, and demonstrated restraint, which pleased her tutor greatly. Dottie looked pensive, then looking up determinedly from Tresseld's pages she announced,

"I'm ready!" She then shut Tresseld closed and stood him upright on his plinth.

"Well, now then, so ye're ready now are ye? My, my, my, quiet the impetuous one aren't ye?! There's a wee bit more to it than that me girl, ye still have to memorise the magic word before ye close me pages and head off into the wild blue yonder, so you can open me back up now and memorise, memorise, memorise."

Dottie opened back at the page on gaining the power of thought, she read over the instructions and committed them to heart, and finally, she turned to the very next page to read the magic word therein. But all she saw was a whole page entirely filled with seemingly random letters. She could not make head nor tail of it all. She began to try and make sense of it by reading it slowly from the top of the page to the bottom, she focused and concentrated, and tried to pronounce it, and she began to read aloud:

"Laaeaepslealslpaeplllleseeeeessspppellleeeee......." She tried and tried to pronounce it, but she could not remember it all. She tried her level best to not let the word beat her, so she kept concentrating on it until eventually, exasperated, she asked Tresseld for his help. He was not amused,

"I thought not ten minutes ago, ye said ye were ready, slammed me shut, and off on yer merry way. What happened to that wee lassie eh?

I am never going to be able to learn any of this, Tresseld, it's just too hard.

Remember me girl, you are looking for the magic word, be patient, focus, let it come to ye."

Dottie was still confused and frustrated.

"But what does this word mean?" Tresseld was not yielding,

"Well now me girl, if ye want the spell, then ye have to find the magic word yersel', it is, after all, just one wee word, surely ye are able to read one wee word?! Or no?! Keep going, it will soon become apparent once ye just apply yersel' and focus."

Dottie protested,

"It all looks like gobbledegook to me Tresseld."

But even so, the little girl settled down and studied the page of letters and, sometime later, she saw something in the sea of jumble, like a mist lifting, the word "Patience" appeared to her, so she hollered out the word, "PATIENCE!" to Tresseld.

"Good girl, ye've cracked it, now memorise it and go back and re-read what you have to do before you go to Sherastsouth."

Dottie was delighted, bouncing up and down in her chair and proclaiming out loud,

"PATIENCE!!! I FOUND IT!!! PATIENCE!!!"

Tresseld flapped his cover in approval and sounded pleased with both himself and his student, even allowing himself a small chuckle.

"Aye, that ye did lass, that ye did."

"Oh, it'll be great to be back where The Goodness lives," Dottie announced with glee, clapping her hands together with sheer joy at the prospect of meeting him again.

"Yes, that's great, Dottie," Tresseld was expelling a great sigh.

"Are you coming with me to the realm of Sherastsouth, Tresseld?" Dottie asked nervously.

"No, Dottie, but if ye need to, if things become too much for ye, then just think of travelling back here, and ye're

Cheromaack will know what to do, trust it, and it will protect ye. If needs be, ye'll be back here in two shakes of a lamb's tail to me, so don't ye worry one wee bit, just enjoy the journey." On saying that, Tresseld opened up again, and leaned back on his freshly polished stand, with the next pages open for Dottie to continue studying. He reiterated, "Now, just to please yer old teacher, one more time, READ!"

CHAPTER 30

The Power of Thought

The wall clock tick-tocked away the hours. Once she had it all learnt off by heart, Dottie said aloud, "Is it time?" Tresseld replied, "It is." She cleared her mind and thought of her Cheromaack flying to her. In a moment it was all around her, enveloping her. Immediately, Dottie felt braver, stronger, smarter, and safer. She bid Tresseld farewell, took a deep breath, gave him a little wave and then she was off. She flew up and out through the open roof window, high up into the twilit sky, right up there with the birds, who were heading off to bed, taking her up further still, into the ether and flying higher and faster, so fast, she was able to do loop-the loops and zig zags all around the sky. The higher up she went, the faster she was able to dive and then slow it down to soar among the gathering evening clouds. She delighted in joining the murmuration of the starlings. Dottie looked around until she spied the arc of the rainbow then accelerated towards it. The Cheromaack's magical speed allowed her to halt the rainbow's retreat and soon she was gaining on it.

Since she first left Tresseld's classroom back in Nell's cottage, she had dreamt for some time now of being close again to her new friend, The Goodness. They bonded instantly when they had first met, and somehow, from that very first meeting, she knew their friendship would last forever. Dottie arrived outside the door to the realm of Sherastsouth, located at the band of blue light in the rainbow, she knocked once, the gatekeeper answered.

"Hello dear Dottie, we've been expecting you, please do come on in."

When Dottie met the gatekeeper again, she observed her golden light shone even brighter than the last time she was there.

"Oh dear, what's her name? Nell forgot to introduce us the last time," she thought, a little embarrassed.

"Oh, I do apologise," said the gatekeeper, "I forgot to introduce myself, my name is Daniance, Guardian of the Blue Gate and loyal servant of The Goodness." She smiled, and lowered her head to one side, in a manner that was both humble and yet regal.

Dottie was surprised at how Daniance anticipated her social dilemma, but relieved that her deftness avoided any awkwardness.

"Very pleased to meet you again, Daniance," Dottie replied, while thinking, "gosh, she has such lovely hair." Daniance already knew what she was thinking and thanked Dottie for her kindness. Dottie knew that she had to get used to this mind-reading ability, possessed by many in the various realms, but it always took her by surprise at first. As she walked with Daniance, she felt very happy indeed. She cast her eyes on the beautiful surroundings again; it was even more magical than she had remembered from her first visit. The memory of that awful Sherida from Sherastnorth, didn't in any way impact on her wonderful memories of that first visit, as The Goodness shone such a bright light over it so quickly it seemed to her no more than a bad dream.

"Am I too late to see The Goodness today?" Dottie asked.

"Oh, no," replied Daniance, "no one could ever be late here, and he's really looking forward to meeting you again, he'll be helping you with your spell you know."

"Oh goody, Daniance," said Dottie. And then, there he was. Dottie's little face lit up, she was spellbound, she nearly fainted at how beautiful his presence was. She must have been looking at him for such a long time with her mouth open, because as he approached her, he gave her a gentle nudge, and made a breathing sound through his nostrils, then he shut her mouth gently with his muzzle, and just smiled lovingly at her. His golden light radiated, and Dottie too started glowing by just being near to him. She looked at her hands, marvelling at how that light bathed her. She had noticed that Daniance too would glow brighter the closer she stood to The Goodness and felt honoured to be allowed share in that magical radiance. His mane, seemed longer, thicker, and wavier, than before and it had the appearance of pure silk, outshone only by the beautiful white ivory unicorn in the centre of his forehead, that was spectacular with its pearlescent sheen. Each time he destroyed any badness, he became stronger in every way; he derived his power of good from drawing out the bad in others until it was no more. The Goodness was used to the awed deference of good people, and even the enforced respect of the bad, so he found Dottie's lack of guile refreshing. "Hello," she said, as yet too small to reach his neck, he lowered his head to allow her to pat him gently on his brow, "what a lovely boy." Dottie treated him as she would any pony she might meet on the farm, and he tolerated her playfulness, even allowing her to braid his mane and tail. They became lost in one another's company, and for a time, Dottie completely forgot she had important business; to gain the power of mind-reading. What she forgot, was that both Daniance, and The Goodness, already knew why she was there and could hear her every thought. They waited patiently for her to ask about going to The Crystal Mountain. After the initial joy of being back in Sherastsouth, and among such lovely folk once more, subsided, she remembered to ask The Goodness about the mountain and if she could go to seek out the magic there. "We will take you straight there, as you need to seek it out for yourself. We have all been on that journey when we were the same age as you are now, and The Goodness has already granted you permission to go to that most sacred place in all of his realm."

As they made their way over the valleys of this great land, countless herds of horses galloped over the green hills. A delicate, calming perfume abounded, and everything in nature was in perfect harmony with its surroundings. Dottie felt sure that no other realm could equal such perfection, not even her own on its best of days. The Crystal Mountain rose up glowing in the distance, and it looked rather small and far away still. However, it was only when they got nearer to it, that it became the biggest and most graceful giant, reaching high up into the sky. Dottie would never forget this first sight of The Crystal Mountain, so majestic in its snow-capped splendour. It had that same glow, like The Goodness's, and a golden shimmer emanated from it. They landed by a ledge just beneath that hallowed cave, one could feel a sense of the sublime in this fantastic place, and Dottie was, to say the least, more than a little awestruck. Sensing her young charge's apprehension, Daniance took Dottie's little hand in hers reassuringly.

"Here we are now, and we'll walk you up to the opening at the other side of this great place where you must then enter The Cave of Magical Light, and there, resting on a granite plinth you will see the white crystal chalice. Hold the chalice in both your hands and place it high up above your head. We know you have studied hard for this ceremony, so you'll know what to do. We will stand just outside the entrance to the cave, so you have nothing to worry about. The Goodness has granted you receive this great gift, so you have nothing to fear little one."

As Dottie tentatively walked in front of The Goodness and Daniance, she suddenly froze with the overwhelming power of the cave, as she had seen nothing like it ever before from her own realm. She suddenly felt that she didn't deserve to be there. The Goodness just nudged her with the side of his muzzle and snorted. She looked back at him for a moment, he seemed to be smiling at her, so then she knew that he was giving her permission. He, in his way, was telling her she DID belong, she DID deserve to be there. Because she felt his confidence and belief in her, it made it possible for her to proceed. She entered The Cave of Magical Light with such calmness now and was amazed at the interior of the place; a vastly wide, cathedral-like space, shining with an internally bright white light dazzling the many pools of clear water around it. There were pure crystals forming stalagmites and stalactites, looking for all the world like carved pillars of glass. The crystal chalice was right in the centre of it all, placed upon a stone plinth with carved stone steps leading up to it. Dottie climbed up without hesitation and took the white crystal chalice, raised it above her head, and incanted her magic spell:

> *All here,*
> *Swear to tell,*
> *Bind all minds,*
> *All hear,*
> *When the bell chimes.*

She remembered this exactly from Tresseld's teachings, and after she had uttered those magic words, a great shaft of light burst forth from the crystal cup. She then brought the chalice down gently and bowed to it. The chalice seemed energized with all the raw power of the mountain itself. She turned and carefully went back down the steps and proceeded to walk back out to where the others were waiting for her. "Would you like to take a stroll with us Dottie, the water is now ready for you to complete your mind-reading spell," Daniance spoke in such a kind, gentle voice. After a short stroll, they came to another smaller cave opening at the side of the mountain. Inside, was a little babbling brook, with a stream of crystal-clear water running down the side of a rock formation into a pool of glowing light. It poured down into a wider stream where you could hear the pebbles in the water being turned over by its gentle flow. At the edge of the pool, Daniance went on to explain the process. "The water has to be drawn from The Pool of Illumination. You must fill the crystal chalice right up to its brim, while keeping it in both hands. The water in the chalice will turn into a rainbow of colours, just for a moment, then it will turn clear, sparkle brightly. Then you must, once again, recite the spell just at that moment, before drinking the water. All of it is to be consumed in one go. Remember child, not a drop to drip twixt the chalice and the lip," Daniance reminded her. Dottie nodded and did as she said, she performed the spell again:

> *All here,*
> *Swear to tell,*
> *Bind all minds,*
> *All hear,*
> *When the bell chimes.*

Then she carefully drank the water down in one go. After completing the spell, she made her way back to The Cave of Magical Light, climbed the same stone steps, and carefully replaced the chalice back in the centre of the granite plinth. She bowed once again, stepped down, and back out to where she left The Goodness and Daniance. So now, all she had to do was wait. She thought she felt no different to before the spell was enacted, until she heard what sounded like a church bell tolling in the far distance. Then the loveliest sound calling to her, when she looked around no one was speaking. Then Dottie heard Daniance, and she looked directly at her, but she was not speaking.

"It works!" she thought,
"Of course it does, Dottie," Daniance thought-spoke; "This is
how we all received the gift, and now you have received it too."
"Oh, my word, I'm able to hear you," Dottie spoke that aloud,
giggled and held her hand over her mouth to stop speaking her
thoughts. Whilst The Goodness had no words she could hear,
she understood what he was communicating to her, it was fascinating but hard to understand at the same time, how he was
able to do this.
"You're now able to understand him the way we can, you're
very special, little one, this is only the beginning for you," Daniance thought. He put down his great head and beautiful
mane of hair, and Dottie hugged him warmly and stroked his
neck gently, he nudged her side playfully. Daniance lifted Dottie up onto The Goodness's back and they were suddenly up in
the air. As he was soaring and gliding around the skies, she was
able to look around at all he showed her. He flew over great
lakes, tall mountains and quaint villages nestled snugly below
them. There was such great beauty to look down upon in every
corner of this realm, and as she saw more and more the higher
The Goodness soared, she thought,
"This is the most perfect day. I could stay up here forever and
ever."
On they flew, the light breeze blowing through her hair, and
the sun warming her face. Dottie watched as the views went by,
The Goodness, and she, enjoying the fun of gliding through
the sky, and delighting in the sights and sounds of this beautiful realm. Not a care in the world....or so they thought.

CHAPTER 31

Ominous Logic

N ell and Juni had been tracking Mai for quite some
time, and they knew that rescuing her back from the
pull of Sherastnorth was not going to be an easy task.
They had hoped that she would come to her senses in her own
time, but now, they realised this had gone on for far too long.
They needed to act fast and intervene, before it was too late,
and Mai would be lost to them forever. As they travelled
through this bad realm in search of their dear old friend, they
came up against all sorts of malevolent forces. One of the
most insidious were miserable creatures known as, *Underearthers.*

Nell and Juni could hear all the different Underearthers constantly calling out to them. Each one more convincing than the
next. They could be very charming and jolly, or they could act
distressed, like they needed you to help them. Sometimes seeming to be in a very sad and helpless state. Underearthers, were
made up of the most undesirable folk from all the other
realms. Those who had spent their entire lives being nefarious,
mean, and caring for no one but themselves, were turned into
Underearthers. On one particular night of each year, in all of
the realms, the bodies of the wicked were transported to
Sherastnorth through the dreams of very powerful little creatures called, Didles.

The Didles, appeared as unassuming furry, featureless, creatures who lived in the twisted, slithering dark vines of

Sherastnorth. It was the Didles' awesome power, to control nightmares, that was able to populate the murky shallow graves of the realm. Each new Underearther was like a seed, a seed that could persist in the earth for years and years, just waiting for the moment its plaintive cry for help was answered. Once answered, the Underearther would rise up out of the mire, to become a soldier in the army of the undead; ready to create chaos, and badness, at the beck and call of the bad rulers. For Underearthers live a half-life, neither dead nor alive, but in stasis. After a life lived badly, Sherastnorth was the only place they fitted in. The intrepid duo had avoided all the callings from those abject creatures from below the ground.

This dark realm welcomes the bad, so as long as they abide by the tacit rules of *The Circle of Shadows*. Of course, if one was of a malicious persuasion, and with knowledge of the Underearthers, then one might call them out intentionally if wanting to build an army of wrongdoers. The original inhabitants of Sherastnorth were a warring race, and for as long as anyone could remember, were in the habit of calling Underearthers, should a mob be required to try and overthrow the seven badnesses who rule The Circle of Shadows. Above ground, all the newly-called to duty would do their master's bidding for a time. Underearthers themselves never called the remaining ones residing beneath to rise and join their legion, because as always, they desired all the power for themselves alone. It would not take long for them to double-cross whoever had called them up in the first place. This was always the Underearthers undoing, and why the seven bad rulers still held ultimate power over everything and everyone. For as long as there is good magic in all the other realms, then these combined positive energies kept the bad forces of Sherastnorth in check. But this was a precarious state of affairs, for if any imbalance were to occur, then those bad forces would instantly begin building and try to impose themselves outward and creep into other realms.

Sheirda's most recent incursion into the realm of Sherastsouth, witnessed by Dottie when she had been flown around by The Goodness, was the latest attempt at spreading badness to another realm. While Mai admired Sherida's audacity, she felt such attacks were too random and lacking in results.

To gain a real foothold into other realms, Mai believed a grander strategy needed to be employed; one where a massing of bad soldiers could be used to invade and then spread mayhem and confusion into the other realms. Once there, she could control such a marauding army. This rising was Mai's plan; she wanted to be a leader, a powerful queen, feared by all. She knew that the selflessness of good magic would prohibit such ambitions, so she decided to work against the good magic, believing this to be her own choice. She had become so deeply embedded in badness, with the hate she had built up against her old friends, that she was growing more dastardly, and more powerful, with each passing day. As her influence grew, so too did the place itself, in population and violence. A malevolent synergy emerged, drawing in those with bad intent from the other realms like a dark magnet. There was such unrest within the realm that its effect was starting to be felt far beyond Sherastnorth. The more Mai's wickedness manifested itself, the more disruption and terror that occurred. Factions were rising up; each trying to gain more and more ground over the others by forming alliances, but then betraying one another so they too could attempt to overpower Mai and crush her. Each faction craved power and desired total domination over the realm of Sherastnorth. It was becoming a seething cauldron of subterfuge, where violence held sway. Mai somehow revelled in all this mayhem, as the more chaotic it was becoming the more powerful Mai was growing. Sherastnorth was already an inhospitable place, desolate; previously green foliage was now replaced by a deep, charred, blackened growth with endless shades of the colour, black. There was a purplish-black, a bluish-black, a brownish-reddish-black, in fact, all the shades of black and burnt tones. The blackened vegetation continued sprouting up everywhere and uprooting itself from the solid ground, the plants themselves could now move freely. They would weave and coil like snakes. The plants could wrap their vines tightly around any unwary creature that wandered too near, winding their tentacles tight and swallowing them up whole. The Underearthers would grab at the roots and hold them still to gnaw on. For the Underearthers, this was their only enemy, but ironically, also the source of nutrients they needed, it was enough to keep their perished bodies in a state of wretched preserve. With this constant gnawing at the roots, the violent foliage would continually trash around in the putrid air, making a communal eerie noise that sounded like screeching wild animals caught in some torturous snare. These dreadful sounds were ubiquitous throughout the entire realm. Their calls might sound like the soft sobbing of a child, at other times, like the sorrowful whimpering of a puppy, constantly trying whatever they could to lure you in. There was no trick they would not attempt in order to fool unsuspecting folk. The two fearless travellers kept their steely focus, whilst journeying in total silence, through this constant sea of noise.

"She's answered all their calls hasn't she, Juni?" Nell thought, disappointed with Mai's newfound wicked ways.

"Yes, she seems to be behind all the changes around here. I can never recall a time when the atmosphere was this thick with menace," Juni replied nodding. They were both taken aback by how powerful the bad energy had become since they last visited. Nell knew most of the Underearthers only too well, as many had been both Juni and Nell's foes in their previous bad lives a very long time ago. But now, they were developing new powers, the likes she had never witnessed before.

On they went, carefully ignoring the Underearthers' callings. Step-by-step they made their way nearer to the *Mountain of Moarte*.

In Sherastnorth's long and complex history, there had been many different dwellers in residence over different eras. The current population were a loose conglomerate of quarrelsome beings called, *Curlocks*. Nell and Juni knew that the best way to find the hidden city of *Neslock,* was to follow some Curlocks, and the best place to find some of these beings was near the base of the Mountain of Moarte.

CHAPTER 32

The Rise of the Curlocks

They had to get to the centre of Neslock, the Curlocks' main city, and the place where Mai was residing. She was a guest of Sherida's, one of the seven bad rulers who reigned over the realm of Sherastnorth and had done so for eons. There had been many rulers before the seven, until Sherida formed an alliance that took the realm into a bitter and protracted war. In the end, the many became just seven, and the battle was so ferocious it threw the entire realm into darkness and chaos. When Sherida was a young girl, she was known to all as Volti, the only child and heir to the throne of Salmakti; a great and fair ruler at a time when Sherastnorth was a young and promising realm. Unbeknownst to her father, his daughter's mind was being poisoned by both her mother, Salmakti's estranged queen, Jelusi, and Volti's grandmother, Asheeda. They worked together to nurture a malevolent desire in the young princess to overthrow her father and seize control of his kingdom. Volti watched her father's benevolent rule, and his happy and loyal subjects, with a growing disdain. It sickened her and, and as she grew older, encouraged by her mother and grandmother, the desire to overthrow him grew deep within her. She became as bad as he was good. Volti bided her time, she schemed, and plotted. She honed her battle craft, and fooled her father with smiles and faux respect, but secretly, she harboured that ambition to usurp the king and seize power. To this end, she dedicated herself to learning bad magic, knowing this would be the key to bringing her plan to fruition. She grew in stature and power, she watched and waited, until, one day, when she felt the time with ripe, she struck, and her father was unseated. He loved his daughter so much; he never suspected the badness inside of her. She claimed his throne, and she changed her name to Sherida, to honour her grandmother's wishes, and so began her reign of terror from her citadel deep in the heart of Neslock.

When Sherida was a young girl, she was known to all as Volti, Neslock was an awfully treacherous place indeed, but very hard to find. It used resonance to cloak itself from any goodness. The Curlocks were unaffected by this resonance but not one of them could be trusted. Nell and Juni needed to be sure that they were heading into the heart of Neslock, and to reach Mai as quickly as possible, whilst also trying to avoid any danger. They knew any conflict they might engage in, even in defence, would only add more energy to fuel the badness in the realm, so they needed to tread very lightly indeed. No matter which way one turned, conflict was ubiquitous in the chaos of Sherastnorth. Nell had her Cheromaack around her, as did Juni, so both were completely protected and invisible, therefore, they were as well prepared as they could be for all eventualities.

As they neared the Mountain of Moarte, they noticed a very scraggly-dressed Curlock. He was leaning on a rock, eating something in a way that made him look like he had never eaten anything before in his life. He was very thin, short, and had dark circles under his very black eyes. His complexion was the colour of an Egyptian mummy and he intermittently chewed something and smoked a very long, thin pipe. All the time he coughed and spat on the ground. An ill-mannered individual if ever there was one. He started to walk along the path, suddenly he turned as if he had the feeling he was being observed, he sniffed the air whilst he looked all around but could not see an-yone, and so, shrugged his shoulders and continued on his way.

When he saw a fellow Curlock walking towards him, he put this feeling of being watched from afar down to him. He never suspected for a moment that he was under the scrutiny of the invisible Nell and Juni. He put his hand up in salute; this was the way Curlocks greeted one another, a semi-militaristic gesture, but performed with all the sloppiness and lacklustre known to the Curlock alone. But as Curlocks were always spoiling for a fight, they would stop fellow travellers and ask them where they were going, and what business they were on, just to seek any possible opportunity for conflict. Curlocks were by nature extremely confrontational.

Nell and Juni listened in on the two while keeping at a safe distance. Curlocks could smell and sense more than most and were keen hunters of anything that moved. They usually hunted alone but had been known to hunt in packs when it was expedient to do so. As Nell and Juni read their minds, they both felt sickened at what they could hear from the Curlocks' twisted thoughts. When Nell heard the first Curlock, Ade, mention Mai by name, she knew that she had to keep a close eye on him to see if he would lead them straight to her. Ade, and his associate were meandering along, closely, and invisibly, followed by Nell and Juni. Farther along the rocky and twisting roadway they encountered a third Curlock, and again, both Ade and his associate put up their hands in salute but also to hinder the progress of this new Curlock.

"What hey?" said Ade.

"What Ho?!" replied the new Curlock. They all knew they were going to get into a fight just for the sake of it, as was their way. The two Curlocks instinctively knew that they wanted to beat up the third just for fun. However, he just smiled back at them with a really strange expression on his face, walked straight over to Ade, squared right up to him only a hair's breadth from his nose, and looked him straight in the eyes. It seemed to Nell and Juni that this standoff had gone on for an age, but suddenly, all three backed off and laughed. All the while, each calculating how hurt they were prepared to get. Instead, they formed an unsteady alliance to go into the city to look for lesser victims that they could beat up and bully into doing their bidding. As Ade spoke, the leftovers of what he had been eating earlier dribbled down his very grimy moustache, somehow making him even more loathsome. He laughed at nothing in particular then pronounced,

"When I look around and see our realm being taken over again by a challenger to the bad rulers, especially that new one, Mai and her accomplices, I am sickened to my guts. I have seen this happen so many times before; it always starts with the one or two of them, but then it builds and builds. NO MORE! I say. We are not going to allow our realm to be ruled by this newcomer, Mai, PAH! Who does SHE think she is?!!" After a slight pause, one of the Curlocks tried to answer him, not quite understanding the niceties of rhetoric.

"M..m.. maybe she thinks…" but Ade just raised his hand and slapped him out of the way.

"Follow me, let us gather up as many of our kind as we can and build a great army of Curlocks."

His small audience seemed to urge him on with grunts and growls.

"When this army rises, then….THEN we will have real POWER to go up against this new force residing here under Sheirda's protection. Why should we stand for it anymore?" Ade reiterated, and proclaimed to the other two, who cheered and nodded in agreement; Curlocks will cheer and nod at almost anything, mind you. Unbeknownst to themselves, Nell and Juni had just witnessed the beginnings of, 'The Rise of the Curlocks.'

As they travelled farther along the path, and passed by some moving vines, they could hear screeching and Didles giggling at the prospect of having more nightmares to dish out to the inhabitants. These Didles liked to live in the vines and think up nightmares; they would spend all their waking hours doing so. They never slept themselves and were in a permanent state of anger and delirium. Growling one minute, then breaking down in manic giggles the next. They vacillated between these two states of being. Curlocks were inured to all this as they enjoyed nightmares and looked forward to the latest one the Didles conjured up for them. Curlocks and Didles got on like a house on fire. Ade thought it useful to use them as a weapon against Mai. His plan was to use the Didles nightmare-creating powers to confuse, weaken, and then overpower her. They wanted to rebel against Mai's rule, and pledged, as best they could, that they would only be loyal to do Sherida's bidding. They knew that even the Trenics she controlled, could be lured away, and would do their bidding. They were timid creatures and were naturally scared of the Curlocks anyway.

"These vile creatures will lead us directly to Mai. We need to keep upwind of them at all times as we follow them into Neslock," Nell thought, with total distrust of them.

Ade knew it was time to make alliances, he wiped his mouth, and he formally introduced himself to the other two Curlocks. It being in the nature of Curlocks, all three were already plotting, in a most dim-witted way, how to overthrow each other. The other two were named Ja and Spn. Ade wiped his hands on the front of his jacket, while thinking how useful this alliance might turn out to be, and unbeknownst to the other two Curlocks, Ade had other plans entirely. So off they went with Nell and Juni in hot pursuit. They came to the outer wall of the city; it was full of holes and had partly collapsed. Debris was strewn all over the place. The denizens were not in the least bit tidy, and just threw everything anywhere. Total disorder that, over the centuries, built up mountains of rubbish from their filthy bad habits. But all the while, quietly, invisibly, Nell and Juni followed.

CHAPTER 33

The Fall of the Curlocks

A s they were being led into the bowels of the city, every-where they looked was full of misery and violence. It was such a scary, foreboding place; the buildings were in a terrible state, many without roofs, their skeletal, burnt timber beams exposed and rotten. It was hard to find any that offered proper shelter. Fires burned in many of the structures, and every sort of lament could be heard echoing around the streets and back alleys. The vines were slowly slithering, moving between the buildings, seeking out any morsel they could squeeze the life out of, and screeching as they moved torturously along. Nell suspected there was something was not quite right about following Ade, worrying that he may be leading them astray. She confided her concerns to Juni, who agreed, but knew they could not stand idly by and let Mai destroy herself. This was part of an oath they had sworn in their initiation ceremonies; to protect one another, no matter what, and to the very end. Both Juni and Nell still loved and cared about Mai despite all her wrongdoings. They could not, and would not, give up on her. As they made their way along the streets, Ade was leading them right to the centre of the city, he pointed to a decrepit old building and turned to address his two fellow Curlocks:

"This is where I will be holding my meeting. Gather as many beings as you both can to attend, and we shall build an army against this interloper. She is residing in the place called the

Lair of the Shadows, heavily guarded against intruders, and I'm reliably informed, that she doesn't like to be disturbed when she's taking her mid-morning nap," he said with a laugh. "We must gather every Curlock from the realm. Go, find every Curlock you can and tell them about this army I'm amassing. We shall not be divided and with our combined strength we will sort her out for all Curlocks, so go, GO find every Curlock! For if we stick together, if we fight for one another, and if we put our trust in the Curlock brotherhood, then we cannot fail," he said. Even as those last words left his mouth, Ade could already feel the enthusiasm waning from himself, Spn and Ja. Once again, the Curlocks innate disloyalty, combined with an inherent apathy, would be their undoing. Ade led the way to spread the word that all Curlocks were having this important gathering, and the three disbanded to find some more Curlocks.

However, as they were leaving, they had forgotten what was said, and got distracted by other things. Ade instinctively knew his plan would never work as intended; Curlocks could never be loyal to anyone, so he was thinking of what he could get out of this for himself. Even during his speech, he had already lost interest in the whole campaign. Curlocks were a disloyal and disorganised lot.

"Let's be on our guard here, Juni, just in case things don't go as expected, their disorder makes them unpredictable, " Nell thought-spoke. Juni acknowledged with a nod of her head. They waited by the wide old wooden door leading into the building, it was not long before all sorts started shuffling up to its entrance. Word travels fast in this realm, and before long the place was teeming with all types; there were Curlocks, Trenics, and even the odd Didle, along with Underearthers moaning and groaning, all gathering to see what they could get out of this for themselves.

The smell was really unbearable to Nell and Juni, but they waited it out to see what the assembled masses would be proposing to do, hoping that this was a way to track down Mai. Ade was surprised with the turnout and was about to get up to make another, spur-of-the-moment, rallying, venomous, speech, but he might as well have said nothing at all, as the mob started to charge and practically ran over him to get ahead of him, as all they thought now was that there might be a bit of trouble in it for them, which they craved. Soon, they were all on the march to The Lair of Shadows with Nell and Juni in pursuit. All the while, as they marched along, no one quite understood how Ade's idea was actually going to work, especially Ade himself. After all, they had no magic to speak of, they were just a mob.

Dust and debris were churned up by the rabble as they gathered. Then, they used their brute strength to knock down the doors of their long-time rulers' residence. They came to a circular opening, which was made from solid rock, and everyone was pouring through it to get inside this lair. Juni felt unsure about following them in, but Nell decided to take the risk, and so, they too headed through with all the others. Everything was pitch black inside, devoid of all light. The foul smell was all they had to track, eventually they could see a shaft of light in the far distance. What they saw at the other side was incredibly ugly, terribly shady, and awfully bereft of any kind of happiness at all as far as they could see.

"How do these rulers live like this?" thought-spoke Juni to Nell. It was packed with all the realm-dwellers, pushing, and shoving past each other. Ade was out in front, ready to storm the thick, dark castle walls. Everyone climbed over each other eventually getting to the top by forming a long Curlock chain festooning up the walls.

By now, Nell and Juni had flown up into the rafters and watched what was going on inside this dark and gloomy fortress. Foreboding wooden doors led to hallways, with more great wooden doors opening out into even more corridors. The last of those doors opened on to a courtyard where all seven of the badness's agents had gathered. Their combined powers controlled the Curlocks. Being so untrustworthy, some Curlocks had already confided to the bad rulers about this impromptu revolution in order to win individual favours from them. Trenics were even worse and had sold out Ade for the price of a meal. Ade was the ringleader and would be banished for trying to overthrow them. He was such a Curlock, that he bargained and negotiated with them. He even betrayed himself, tying himself up in knots. He somehow convinced them that his whole plan was a means to serve the badness, and not to overthrow the regime. In the end, he wept, and pleaded, whined, and fawned, and was now begging them to help him end his own feeble revolt. The Badness's agents could have wiped him out in a split-second, but they knew that he would come in handy to do their bidding. The Rise of the Curlocks was over, and with immediate effect, the rabble were now working for the bad agents.

CHAPTER 34

Mai's Trap

T hen Mai appeared, shining dimly, the last vestiges of her good power still aglow in the bleakness. She had eyes as black as the night, and they were emitting a strange light that shone out to where the invisible Nell and Juni were hiding. Now, caught in the beams of this strange light, everyone could see the two of them; their invisibility was exposed. What were they to do? All the assembled mob were looking directly at them. Some of the mob could fly also and so Nell and Juni were surrounded. The non-flying beings below in the courtyard roared up at them shaking their fists.

"I know what brought you two here, you thought that both of you could save me," Mai said, with a vindictive laugh. She flew up and faced them. She looked so different now to how they remembered her, so different to how she looked only a short time ago.

"Oh Mai, you have us all so worried about you. Please come back home with us. We all miss you dearly, and need you back safe," Nell pleaded.

" Oh dear, oh dear, oh dear," said Mai ominously. "So, you two witches thought you were coming here to rescue me from myself, did you?! Oh, how delicious!" Mai started to chortle a tad uncontrollably. "My dear deluded old crones, I am not the one that needs rescuing….such arrogant fools…YOU are the only ones in mortal danger here! How kind of you to care so much, how nice, how saccharin. I'm here of my own volition and want to remain here. I'm not going back with either of you, NEVER," she hissed, with such hate and bitterness in her voice.

They both tried the direct approach by pleading with her, to see the error of her ways, but it really didn't seem to work.

"I tried to explain it to you nicely, but since you're so insistent, then you leave me no choice but to show you just how I feel about the two of you." She suddenly moved her hands up, and with an almighty sound, she gathered all her strength against her two oldest friends. Mai used her newly-acquired terrible powers to surround them with such a great, and bad, force that they found themselves trapped in a vortex. She had them both surrounded by a trap so powerful that Nell and Juni knew that they could not free themselves from it. Both had never before felt such a mighty force, all the beings that Nell had banished with Drackon were now freely swirling around them and combining all their powers with Mai's. Nell recognised every single one of them, and they too recognised her, as each one passed around her, smirking and glowering at her. She could see in their eyes that it was pure hate and revenge fuelling their power.

They both struggled with their Cheromaacks but seemed to be powerless to do anything at all. Whatever force Mai was using had rendered the magical cloaks completely redundant. By trusting their old friend, they had let their guard down, thinking they could reason with her. But this was not the same old friend they had once known, not that same Mai that they had trained with as children. It was too late now to protect themselves, and they somehow had to send out a distress message to the other realms. This combined attack on them was just too strong, and they now suspected that they had been set up by Mai. She made sure that they were well and truly caught in her trap. Nell and Juni combined and channelled all their energies to send out as powerful a message as they possibly could. The message was only one, solitary, word….

"HELP!"

Then they felt their own cloaks suddenly wrap tightly around and about them, tighter and tighter until they were totally bound up, and it felt a little difficult to breathe. Nell looked to Juni and thought-spoke,

"Hold strong and keep believing," and then they both closed their eyes and appeared to fall into a state of deep unconsciousness. This very powerful badness had turned their Cheromaacks against them it seemed. Never before had either of the sorcerers encountered such behaviour from their own Cheromaacks.

The two women slowly floated downwards to the floor where Mai's minions grabbed them and carried them off to the dungeons. There, in those awful dungeon cells, the thick quartz walls would act as barriers to any attempts by Nell and Juni to send out telepathic calls for help. Neither would they be able to use their magic to escape. All seemed lost.

Mai had become a vision of pure badness, once she had been a great and pure beauty, the one destined to be the greatest of all the crystal sorcerers. She was a guiding light, and an inspiration to all others, but her great power and goodness came at a cost. The stronger her power for good grew; the bigger the prize she became to those who would do her wrong. For the bad powers to grow, they needed to feed off goodness, and the greater Mai became with her good powers, the more attractive she was to the denizens of Sherastnorth. But that now seemed like a long time ago. Gone were her clear and sparkling blue eyes, replaced instead with a blood red colour, devoid of any kindness. Everything about her was deeply gloomy, her skin had taken on a greenish tinge, she seemed to have absorbed all the badness around her and drew it inside of her, replacing all that was once so pure and good. Her now darkened powers had dimmed her light until it was almost extinguished.

All sorcerers know of the serious challenges ahead as their knowledge of crystal magic deepens; the more they learn, the more powerful they become, they in turn become an attractant for those who practice the bad powers. Their good powers can be tapped by those who seek to do wrong and warped to ply their dastardly trade. A day comes for all those initiated into the Council of the Realms, when that balance between good and bad is challenged. Those who practice good magic will begin to seek out the bad; it draws them in and becomes a compulsion in them. This is why each practitioner of crystal magic swears an oath to look out for the signs of it in each other. They promise to never forsake one another during this time known as *The Turning*. They vow to fight with all their being, and with every ounce of their magic, to save their colleagues who are in danger of being swamped by the badness. With the right help, it can always be overcome, however, with Mai it was different. Her goodness had been so strong that her transition to the badness was profound. She had lost all sense of who she once was, and truly believed she had the power to control it and denied all need to be helped. Because the bad knows this about the good, the moment Mai was nearing her time for The Turning, they were ready to pounce.

As with all sorcerers, travelling through Sherastnorth on the odd occasion to do sorcerer business, the common practice was normally to travel in pairs. This pair comprised of one experienced sorcerer and one novice, so that, at the first sign of it taking one of them, it can be quickly noticed and quelled. Over time, and with subsequent controlled exposure, a type of immunity builds up, and the ability of the bad power to supplant the good is weakened.

In Mai, her great natural abilities had perhaps imbued her with an overconfidence, she had grown complacent to the dangers, and she felt she could go in there on her own and remain unaf-fected. Slowly, almost imperceptibly, the bad in her grew. Each time she would go back in, she was not able to detect it hap-pening to her, and so its hold on her grew stronger and stronger. By the time it was realised how serious it had become, she had been swallowed up by it, and she now was doing their bidding freely convinced it was out of choice.

Mai came into the cold dungeon to oversee her two old friends being secured to the enchanted iron shackles. No trickery or magic could unlock those rusty chains. She started to laugh mockingly and stated,

"You should never have come in here," her voice echoed loudly through the dismal corridors. She moved closer to them, smirk-ing at their pitiful plight, and in her eyes, there was pure hatred. "I'm really quite enjoying being nasty and wicked," she said, with a wry smile. "The life I lived with all that kindness and goodness was destroying me, do you hear? It was sucking the very life out of my bones. I can honestly say, Nell, my very old and dear friend, with my hand on my withered and cold heart, I've never felt more contentment and satisfaction since I de-cided to dwell here in Sherastnorth. I'm never leaving, I can tell you that. You will not get out of here alive if you utter another word about making a mistake or choosing the wrong path. Who are you two to judge what's best for me? I have been good for eons. I'm just really sick of it all, do you hear?" Her voice could be heard echoing off the damp walls and roaring down all the dank corridors. "I'm just so sick of being GOOD!"

As she bellowed out her fury, her sonic waves flowed from her entire being with all the ferocity and power of a volcano erupt-ing. The force was pushing both Nell and Juni back against the cold cell wall. Through half-opened eyes Nell could see Mai raging. She had never seen such pure anger before. "How do you do it Nell? How are you not sick of it all at this stage, not sick of all that goodness? Being good is all so repetitive." Mai said with such venom and spitefulness being uttered in every single word that she spoke, her eyes narrowing with hate. "Being bad certainly has not improved the company you keep," said Nell defiantly. "You don't know what you're saying Mai, they've you convinced that you came to this decision all by yourself. This isn't you, you would never have chosen this way of life for yourself, not in a million years. Please, Mai, just stop and think about where you are, and what you are doing here" Nell pleaded with her.

"What a load of old poppycock, you deserve to stay trapped in here forever, or till you rot, whichever comes first," Mai spat out and laughed. "I am the very best of the best, no other has ever attained my level of power over the craft. You said so yourself Nell, when I was your apprentice all those years ago. You told me, *I* am the best there ever was, and no other could surpass me!"

Nell's face now looked younger, and her steely gaze held Mai's, "Well, I was *wrong*," said Nell defiantly.

"Hah!" spat Mai, a momentary flicker of doubt seemed to flash across her eyes on hearing her old tutor say those words. She flew off and went in search of poor souls who needed to be introduced to their pure badness. A groggy Juni turned to Nell,

"Did you see how wicked she has become Nell? What are we going to do now? Nell took her friends hand, and in a quiet voice said,

"All we can do now is hope they heard our call for help."

CHAPTER 35

Dottie to the Rescue

Back in Sherastsouth, where The Goodness was showing Dottie around his realm, Dottie suddenly sensed something awful was happening. It felt similar to the chill one might feel when a dark rain cloud obscures the heat of the sun on a summer's day. She felt The Goodness shudder perceptively beneath her.

"Something's not right with Nell," she spoke aloud. Dottie thought she could hear a faint call for help; it sounded just like that of her friend and tutor. Somehow, Dottie and The Goodness both knew Nell was in deep trouble somewhere in the realm of Sherastnorth. She instinctively knew that The Goodness was going to go into that shadowy realm to rescue Nell and Juni. Despite Nell's warning of the great perils Dottie would encounter if she dared to enter that awful place, she did not hesitate, and knew she must go there too. Although she was a child, and magic was all very new to her, she was aware of the very real dangers Sherastnorth posed. It was perilous to sorcerers far older and far more experienced than she was, and yet she felt protected with The Goodness by her side. She, and The Goodness, had to face whatever that frightening realm held in store no matter what. They glided back down to Daniance, who was patiently waiting for them but with a look of grave concern on her face, she too had heard that faint call for help. Seeing even Daniance look so concerned only seemed to add to the gravity of Nell's predicament in Sherastnorth.

Without a single word being said aloud, all concurred that their friends were in imminent danger and were in urgent need of their help.

Dottie had heeded Nell's warning to be very wary of that place, but she was not afraid, she thought she could be of help to The Goodness in some fashion. All she wanted to do was save Nell and Juni from whatever trouble they had found.

In Sherastnorth, the group of seven bad rulers, known as The Badness, were the antithesis of The Council of Realms and thrived on nefarious deeds.

All seven had been excluded a long time ago from being part of the C.O.R. because of their choice to be bad and had been banished to Sherastnorth for eternity. Sherida, the whirling witch, was one of the seven. She was banned from the C.O.R. as she chose to be bad and overthrew her father from his kingdom many eons ago. Her encounter with The Goodness recently had seen her reduced in strength, although only on a temporary basis. She could, of course, choose to mend her ways, but from previous encounters, proved she always reverted to the bad side and always chose badness over the good. For a much of the time, living in their dank isolation, the seven bad rulers were dormant, and did not threaten to expand their field of influence. But recently, their bad energies had combined and strengthened to the point they could now coerce others to aid and deepen their own bad powers. To a young questioning mind, The Badness had the power to overwhelm and then extinguish any good. The Badness fed on the innocent, the kind, and the good.

On entering Sherastnorth, everything is turned upside down. Reality becomes distorted; it becomes hard to tell whether it is the good, or the bad, that is informing your behaviour. The Badness weakened the unwary by confusing them, and it subtly changes those in its thrall. At first, their behaviour starts to slowly change in subtle ways; politeness is forgotten and becoming more aggressive is considered the normal way to behave. This transformation, this confusion, this usurping of the rules of decency, are all fun and games to those seven bad rulers. Since birth, everyone from Sherastnorth participated in this sort of aggressive behaviour, so it dominates every greeting; the more that are on this bad side, the more normal and acceptable this bad behaviour is. All the inhabitants seem autonomous but, in fact, act as if part of one large and nasty mind. In a sometimes-soporific state, and in a most uncoordinated fashion, they do The Badness's bidding and continually wreak havoc in the realm of Sherastnorth.

Dottie could sense The Goodness's thoughts and felt exactly the same as he did. She hoped she had enough magic to help rescue Nell.

Flying on The Goodness's back, they arrived at the door to Sherastnorth in no time at all. Dottie instantly recognised it from her bad dream; when Teddy had protected her and shielded his young charge from the worst excesses of The Badness. It had tried to reach out to her in her dreams. She shuddered and shook off the memories of that horrible nightmare and felt very brave entering this dark and scary doorway. The carvings on the door were dense and twisted around themselves with monsters popping out from behind its structures, sticking out their tongues and growling at the new visitors, sensing their goodness. The carvings were recoiling, covering their eyes, and screeching in a great burning pain. The door changed in shade from black, to green-black, and then back to black again, devoid of any reflections. The two went on unperturbed through to this darkest of all realms. Their full attention was now focused firmly on saving Nell and Juni at all costs. Both Dottie and The Goodness worked as one; steeling themselves as they headed inside. Dottie noted that the doorway into Sherastnorth was one of the deepest she had ever gone through; tunnel-like and slanting downwards in direction. As

Dottie walked along it, she felt something touching her shoulder, and an icy coldness descended around her; the type that would chill one to the bone. Once out the other side, everything changed, they heard all the callings from the Underearthers who were begging them to be raised up. The Goodness snorted with derision and encouraged Dottie to ignore their pathetic cries. Steadfastly, they continued on their way, they knew they must keep focused and block out all distractions, no matter what comes their way. The Underearthers were very compelling, and the unwary could feel at any moment that they might get drawn in and then be lost among the mire.

As a newly minted mind-reader, Dottie struggled at first to block out their callings and thoughts, but soon learned to tune out the countless nasty little voices surrounding her young mind. The Goodness sensed her being drawn in to listen, he helped her to zone it out of her thoughts and use her own way of not listening to any of their pleas. Dottie, while weakened momentarily, now felt strong again and was able to drown them out.

The two of them continued their quest for Nell and Juni going deeper into the realm. Once The Goodness found his bearings he signalled to Dottie and they both took to the air. Looking down they could see the land of Sherastnorth from a height, and it looked even more desolate than from the ground. Before them was a terrible vista; strewn with the debris from all of their horrible wars, a blasted landscape with destruction all around. Gangs of unrecognisable beings constantly attacked each other on the ground below. This chaos was a daily occurrence as each creature was vying for power over any part of this realm. It was a perpetual battle, and the ravages of time were now showing the extent of the damage done to the place since The Goodness was last here. He noted that things were so much worse than before, and he was not seeing signs of things improving any time soon.

Dottie was aware from her history classes of her own realm's
Dottie was aware from her history classes of her own realm's
last great war and all the destruction that it had caused. Her father and mother talked about that time and of how her father's
uncle, Travers, was lost in battle. He was missing-in-action and
presumed dead and this was a source of great sadness to them
all. A silver-framed photo of him sat in pride of place on the
piano in the drawing room. She had heard so many wonderful
things about Uncle Travers from her father; how he had always
brought him little hand-made gifts or chocolates when he was a
lad. He was the kind of uncle Dottie would have loved. From
all accounts, he seemed to have a maturity far beyond his years.
So, when his country called, he had no hesitation in signing up,
and heading into battle, though barely out of his teens. Sadly,
somewhere out there on the battle fields of Flanders, he was
lost and never returned. Now, only that sepia-coloured photo-
graph remained to remind everyone of the great sacrifice he,
and so many others, had made. The Goodness was saddened
by Dottie's memory, as it made Dottie unhappy, to think that
this might have been the kind of place where Travers had gotten lost.

The Goodness projected happier, masking thoughts into Dottie's mind to prevent her from drifting too deeply into melan-
cholia. He knew this was another route The Badness could take
in order to inveigle its way into an unwary young mind.

"On we must go, concentrate, be strong, be brave, and never
give up the resistance to The Badness," she felt The Goodness
impart these thoughts to her. Dottie felt reassured that her
choice was the right one, and to not get drawn into the path
Mai had chosen.

CHAPTER 36

The Four Stones of Moarte

Suddenly, four of the seven bad rulers materialised, they hovered in the air surrounding Dottie and The Goodness. They were combining their forces to try to attack Dottie; they were not so stupid as to take on The Goodness alone and were focusing on his young friend. The Goodness could sense the danger for Dottie, so he drew their attention away from her. Dottie could sense him telling her to make for the nearby village where he would rendezvous with her once he had lured these bad rulers away to a safe distance. Dottie took her chance and used her Cheromaack to fly as fast as she could to the village. As The Goodness flew away from Dottie to divert their attention, he was encircled by the four but in no real danger; their powers faded in his presence. However, his attention was on getting Dottie to safety and he did not realise the four were slowly leading him farther away....he did not notice crossing over the four stones of black Zynite crystal. Four stones mined from the deepest recesses of the Mountain of Moarte. Four powerful stones that Mai had carefully placed there on the moorland earlier that day. These stones emanated a bad energy; they could create a field of power that was now inhibiting the mind-connection between The Goodness and Dottie. An invisible wall between his thoughts and hers. He had lured them deeper into the hinterland of Sherastnorth, but it had come at a cost – his mind connection to Dottie had been severed and before he knew it, Dottie was on her own.

In another part of the realm, from her incarceration in Mai's awful dungeon, Nell sensed Dottie and The Goodness's presence; she knew they had come to try to rescue her and Juni. Nell was deeply concerned for her young pupil's safety. She knew that The Goodness would protect her of course, but she couldn't help worrying, as she had a bad feeling about Dottie arriving at this very dangerous realm at such a young age. She could feel there was a bad force working around both Dottie and The Goodness. Nell wished she could do something to help Dottie herself, but Mai's bad powers were constantly blocking any attempts at unshackling her bonds. It was all down to Dottie and The Goodness now. Nell closed her eyes once again,

"Good Luck little one," she projected this thought as powerfully as she could, hoping it would somehow filter through Mai's dark barriers and reach her young apprentice.

CHAPTER 37

Dottie is Deceived

N ow on her own, Dottie found that the calls of the Underearthers were getting stronger, and bolder, calling out to her. It was really hard not to listen a little bit. She was doing her best to resist, and not to answer them. As Dottie walked down the cobbled street of the village, she saw an old lady leaning awkwardly on a windowsill. She seemed a little lost, and confused, so Dottie felt compelled to find out what was wrong, and if she might help in some way. The old lady turned her face away and asked the child not to pity her. Dottie told the old woman not to be afraid and comforted her. She placed her little hand on the old lady's arm and told her everything was going to be okay; she was sure of it.

"If you will allow me, then I may be able to help you," said Dottie softly.

"You're very kind dear, no one here has ever been so kind to me before, so thank you for caring, but you will never be able to fix what's wrong with me, I'm beyond fixing, but thank you anyway. Where are you headed to little girl?" asked the old woman.

"Oh, we're going to help out a friend so we must be on our way, as long as you'll be ok now?" Dottie asked. The elderly lady didn't want her to leave just yet. Her hand tightened around Dottie's wrist.

"Could you help me up, dear? I'm not as steady on my feet as I used to be these days," she started to chuckle and laugh to herself. Although Dottie was in a hurry, she felt she had to give a little of her time to help this elderly lady out. "I'm so very hungry too, could you get me something to eat? Are you hungry, little one? There's a market over there around the corner, and it's the only place a poor old lady like me can get something to eat. They always have extra food which they give away if they can't sell it. It's just, if I wasn't so boockety I wouldn't ask, but would you mind helping me to get over to it?"

"No, of course, I'd be glad to help," Dottie replied.

"Pardon my manners, what's your name, little one?" As Dottie had wandered off with her, she was widening the gap between herself and The Goodness. She could no longer feel his presence, and couldn't understand why, or where he had got to. Where was he? She was getting worried now. Sensing Dottie's concern, the old lady asked, "What's the matter with you?

"I've lost a friend of mine." Dottie replied.

"Oh, don't worry, I'm sure your friend will turn up again soon," the old lady said sharply, while taking Dottie's hand in hers so she could lean on her as she walked. Unsolicited thoughts came into Dottie's mind as she was beginning to wonder if Sherastnorth was really as bad a place as Nell had warned her. She felt good helping this lady out, so it didn't seem that scary to her at all, anymore. Unbeknownst to Dottie, as they were walking along, a strong bad energy was building around them. Dottie was being led into a trap, the old lady already knew all about Dottie and her plans to save her friends. It was she who was blocking Dottie's connection to The Goodness. What Dottie didn't realise, was that this old lady was really the horrible Mai up to her nasty tricks again.

She knew that while she maintained that invisible shield blocking all of them from The Goodness, this would render Dottie very vulnerable indeed to her wicked ways, and those of her accomplices. Mai knew that behind this shield, she could lure her away from him, and into her safe area where nothing could read her mind.

Dottie had a caring nature, so she couldn't help herself, too young yet to think on her feet, not street smart at all, and was now fully in a trap that would not be at all easy to break out of. She could no longer sense The Goodness's' presence, now she was facing the dangers of this realm all on her own.

Mai had big plans for her, none of them good of course, and couldn't believe her luck when the little girl showed up. While she was no match for The Goodness, or his powers, she had been planning ways of giving him the slip for years. She developed a way of cloaking herself and a small area around her from his detection. So even if he was nearby, he was not able to sense anything from her subconscious. She knew she had to get her prey away from him as fast as she could. Her dastardly crystal shield was only temporary, so she had to lure Dottie away to a safe house which she had lined with her cloaking bad magic. Dottie could hear voices all around her and she was unable to block them out, there were just too many people to help, and her head was in a spin.

As they got nearer and nearer to the market an older man was waiting for them and he gave them some food from his stall. "She's a regular here, she is, Old Ma, we call her."

"This is Dottie, Mani, Dottie, meet Mani, she is so kind to help me, isn't she?"

"Pleased to meet you Dottie, and yes, what a thoughtful little girl, yes, really thoughtful, ha, I might as well take my break now, how about we all take a little walk, and I can make you all a lovely glass of lemonade back at my place?" he said, giving Old Ma a sly look.

Dottie started to worry that The Goodness was nowhere to be found and began to wonder about the market stall owner, Mani. Dottie was looking forward to the glass of lemonade, the old man was quite insistent, and she did not want to appear rude, so she went along to his house while helping the old lady. Once there and had made sure the elderly lady was safely at the door, she thanked them both for their hospitality, made her apologies for needing to leave directly, and said she wanted to go back to find her friend. But they convinced her to come inside for a while, it would not do for her to just leave so suddenly; all they wanted was a little of her time, and a chat by the fireside.

Just outside the broken-down fence of Mani's home a young woman greeted them and asked to join them. She too said she wanted to assist this kindly old lady, and to escort them all back inside. This act of charity seemed to annoy the old woman and Mani,

"Hi there, any news from you two? Who do we have here?" she asked looking at Dottie. "Hello," she said, "and what brings you here child?" She continued talking, not allowing Dottie to speak and filled the time with all her news, and even though they seemed to find the young woman really annoying, they let her come with them. She was asking all sorts of questions of Dottie, and chatting away with her, she seemed friendly. Dottie took to her straight away, and was glad to chat to her, inexplicably, Dottie felt safer with this stranger than she did with Mani or the old lady. "I'm Volti," said the stranger. Volti was, in fact, Sherida's alter-ego, a kinder, gentler version of her usual bad personality. She had become so suppressed by her recent encounter with The Goodness, that she had temporarily forgotten all her nasty ways and, for a time at least, a softer nature had emerged. She had all the demeanour of a rather decent and kindly being. The Goodness had been too strong for Sherida, and she had flown too close to his cleansing light. She thought the earlier find of a rare protection herb from the realm of Vilshoct, by a Trenic, would make a guarding potion that would shield her from the light of The Goodness. But she was mistaken. Instead, his light had seared the badness right out of her.

It would be many months before her alter ego Volti faded, and for Sherida's character to dominate once more.

There was a tension in the air, and it was clear Mai and Mani did not want to invite Volti in. They suggested that Volti must be busy and have little time to spare. They seemed keen to have Volti leave them. Reluctantly, Volti said she had better go, but before she left, she looked Dottie in the eyes and said, in a familiar voice, "Good luck little one!"

Once inside Mani's house everything suddenly changed; the atmosphere felt decidedly chilly, Mai turned to Dottie and introduced herself.

"My name is Mai; you've probably heard about me from your friend Nell?" Mai no longer looked like the old lady Dottie had stopped to help, and all that talk of lemonade was just a trick to get her into the house. Dottie was annoyed that she had been duped, but also that she would not be getting some delicious lemonade.

"You lied to me. How could you be so mean?" Dottie asked. Mai just smirked at her little captive, then cocked a sneer at her before turning to speak to Mani. Soon their voices were raised, and Mani started arguing with Mai. The two of them left the room and continued to argue about something just out of earshot.

"What was all that about? You told me it would be secure. I thought that dungeon was secure, you heard what Volti had said just there, that was not her speaking just now. That was Nell, channelling through her, to get a message to her little minion. You told me those dungeons were impervious to magic. I know my two prisoners are not in a secure place and this is all your fault!" Her voice became harsh and started to sound cruel, spewing vitriol. She seemed lost in her anger. She railed and spat at Mani, getting louder and louder. He could not stay quiet, and they were attacking one another ferociously,

"Well, it blocked your magic, didn't it? Maybe she has better magic than you," he retorted.

Dottie, now alone in the back room, slowly backed away until she found an unlocked door-handle. It opened an old creaky door and she tried to make her escape. Dottie found herself in a long corridor leading to a set of stairs, as she climbed it, she could hear their voices dampen down a little with each step. Mai and Mani had turned on one another, and there was a terrifying screeching sound coming from both. Their argument sounded monstrous and vicious. Even when Dottie reached the top of the stairs, she could still hear them arguing, their shouting muffled by the distance. There were doors into two other rooms, so she turned the handle of one and peaked inside. She saw a bed with a dresser and bare wooden floorboards, with a threadbare old rug, so she went in and closed the door quietly behind her and started to look around, trying to find some way out. There was nothing else in this room, so she glanced out the barred window, and saw nothing but destruction all around. Nell was right, this was an awful place, Dottie thought to herself. She recognised that when Volti had wished her good luck, it was Nell who was speaking through her. She was not afraid now; she had a mission, and she knew she had to get away from this place and fast. Suddenly, someone was at the bedroom door, Dottie could hear a metal key turning in the lock and outside the door Mai muttered in a sinister mocking fashion,

"Your mother said you're not going anywhere little girl," followed by an insane cackling and snorting. All was changed now; Dottie was well and truly trapped.

She was left there for a few hours before Mani could be heard turning the key in the lock. He gave her some stale bread and water to eat. He left the room giggling to himself and locked that door after him. How would she get away from them? She didn't know, as none of her magic was working at all. Even her little spells were not working, she was shut in this little room with very little in it and only a little mouse in the corner looking at her, so she tried to change it into a cat, but nothing worked. She started to doubt herself and her abilities which frustrated her greatly. She thought they must have put some kind of a spell on her, all her calling to her Cheromaack was useless, nothing could hear her in that house.

Dottie knew she had to stay strong and plan her escape, as she thought, if she could just get away from them, she had a chance of using her Cheromaack again to fly away from their nasty clutches.

Dottie wondered, "What are they going to do to me? I can't let Nell down now in her hour of need." But everything she was thinking Mai could hear. She burst in the door, laughing at the little girl, she was no longer old, and Dottie felt like crying. She had been tricked and behind her captor was, Mani, who now looked like a very nasty monster; his eyes so dark and his face so cruel-looking. She knew she had to fake her own thoughts now so they would not hear her real ones. She had to distract them from what they were going to do with her. Dottie knew she was in terrible trouble all right, she just had to wing it with them, as they could hear every plan she was trying to think up. "Nell said you were in trouble—she came to save you, and instead you trick me and have done something mean to your oldest friend. How could you prefer this awful place? How could you cause such terrible trouble? How could you?" asked Dottie. "Look here child, you are the only one in trouble here—this is a great place to live, we get to do whatever we like and anything we want, you can have everything here too Dottie. You don't need anyone telling you what to do, or how to do it when you live here. Join us. We are winning over the other realms, they all want to be with us, and live like us, and even your own one is going back to war again. Why go back to such a place? There is always so much corruption and struggle back there. Join us and you could be a ruler here when you get older. We have everything you could ever dream of; JOIN US!" Dottie tried not to think about what she was really thinking, but acted a little mesmerized, as if swayed by Mai's entreaties. Dottie thought, "Yes, why not join them?" Dottie filled her head with thoughts about joining Mai and living in Sherastnorth. It would be the end of rationing for her, and all she really wanted was all the sweet things she could eat, and she wanted them now. On hearing this, Mai felt she was winning one more recruit away from Nell and The Council of Realms. After a day or so, Mai believed Dottie was truly turning towards the way of badness, so she took the child out to a sweet shop and she feasted her eyes on every imaginable sweet that was ever invented and more, it was amazing, and Dottie was able to get everything.

"This is great. Nell must have gotten it all wrong, this is the greatest day ever," Dottie thought to herself. This pleased Mai greatly, felt she could trust Dottie now and was almost a little disappointed at how easily this supposed gifted child was to fool.

"Like taking candy from a baby," said Mai, under her breath.

"Ha, too right Mai," said Mani, now entering the sweet shop and grabbing handfuls of sweets then shoving them in his mouth rudely.

"We have a fine new recruit, don't we? Now we can release more Underearthers with her help. This realm will become the strongest one in the whole rainbow, and all will bow down before us by the time we're finished releasing all of them since right back to when the first one arrived here," Mani roared, laughing uncontrollably, and let half-chewed sweets and drool fall from his mouth.

"We, Mani? You speak a lot about this *we* business. Might I remind you that it is *I* who will be ruling this realm and you will obey me, and *only* me, do I make myself clear?"

"Very clear Mai, sorry, ma'am. I lost the run of meself there, ma'am," Mani hissed, feeling a little annoyed at being taken down a peg or two, but also still fearful of her ire.

"Ok Mai, I'm in, I will do whatever you would like me to do for you? But first, I'm feeling really bloated from eating all those sweets and my tummy hurts," Dottie announced, clutching her tummy.

"You can walk it off, as we go to Neslock," Mai snapped at her sharply, as she could barely tolerate children at all, only tolerating Dottie because she could feel her store of innate magical power, which Mai hoped to tap and use to her own advantage. "Now stop your whinging and come with me.

CHAPTER 38

Dottie's Break for Freedom

A s they walked along the dusty, windy way in the direction of the city, a very powerful looking woman suddenly appeared in the middle of the road. She was dressed in warrior clothes and wielding a great sword. It was a powerful magic sword, given only to those who had proven themselves in battle. The sword was a sign that this woman was a great fighter from the original realm of Sherastnorth. Long before The Badness took hold, or the Underearthers were laid to their unrest, Sherastnorth had been the home of a proud warrior folk. Mai stopped and greeted her with a great deal of respect, while almost bowing, she had lost all her angry and grumpy demeanour. Mai introduced her to Dottie as the great and powerful warrior of the realm, "Shala." She had fought alongside all the best warriors, in all the great wars. In battle, she was always at the front and always ready to die, she was a legend among all in the realm. Even Mai respected her greatly and was very careful with her, knowing Shala could quickly turn on you and have it in for you. Mai knew it was best to always keep on Shala's right side.

Shala took to Dottie straight away; she sensed a kindred warrior spirit, and her keen instincts wanted to protect the little girl from Mai. The warrior joined them on their journey down the road to Neslock, to find out what Mai's plans were for this little warrior girl. All around them there were Underearthers' voices calling out to them, and Mai was answering as many as she could, each one rising up and following her. Each newly raised being forming a part of her ever-growing army. Mani, a Curlock by birth, seemed to be doing the same only not as many were rising with him. He was slow to answer all calls, however, they were both looking at Dottie now to see what she was going to do, and if she would respond to any of the Underearthers' calls.

Dottie was scared but tried not to let it show. What was she supposed to do? Mai guided her into responding to each one in her own way and to help them. Then Dottie heard Shala thinkspeak to her,

"Fear not brave one, there are still a few of us good ones left." She encouraged Dottie to make good her escape as she would distract the other two. Mai could not detect the warrior's thoughts as Shala's gifts were ancient. She had the ability to focus her thoughts, so finely, that she was able to send them directly to Dottie without being overheard. This was Dottie's best chance; she had to trust Shala to help her get out of this terrible situation.

In the meantime, not realising that Dottie and Shala were communicating and planning her escape, Mai was chastising Dottie for being so slow to answer the calls from the Underearthers. Dottie played for time by acting a little naïve, she knew what to do but she just was not able to respond, not the way they were doing it.

"I'm not sure how to do it? Are they not happy where they are?" Dottie asked an increasingly irritated Mai.

"You'll answer them when they call you, that is all you have to do. Duh! Some might not want to follow us but if they hear a child answering them then they will be more encouraged to follow."

This scared Dottie but she knew her back was up against the wall, she couldn't leave Mai or Mani see that. She had to be strong and stay sharp. Dottie heard Shala thought-speak to her,

"Be ready now child. On my mark, I want you to run, run as fast and your legs will carry you, and get distance between you and these two. Once you are far enough away, your powers will return, and you will once again be able to hail your Cheromaack." Dottie nodded subtly, being careful not to look as if she and Shala were in contact. The warrior woman suddenly seemed to get angered by one of the stumbling and barely awake Underearthers,

"Unhand me you miserable cur!" Shala commanded, placing her right hand on her sword's hilt, as if threatening to draw it from its scabbard.

All who knew of Shala's history were aware that once her sword was drawn it would not be sheathed again until it had tasted flesh and blood. All were scared, even Mai and Mani. "Now child, run, run like the wind," Shala commanded.

Even before Shala's words ended, Dottie was already running like a hare down the muddy roadway. The place was very misty, cold, and damp. She could hardly see in front of her nose, but she knew she had to keep running. She had to put enough distance between Mai, and her power to suppress Dottie's magic that blocked the link between her and The Goodness. Dottie ran but also called to her Cheromaack, she must get it back, she must find The Goodness, and she must help save Nell.

Mai and Mani were now fully distracted by Shala, who was blocking her from hearing the advice she had been giving Dottie, they were busy with their new recruits, and this was Dottie's best chance to get away from the two of them before they noticed she was gone. Dottie hoped, that if she could get as far away from Mai as possible, then The Goodness would hear her again and he would come and save her. So, she persevered, heading off past the Underearthers and would not believe or listen to any of them. Having fallen for Mai's trick, she knew now that they were all not to be trusted. She was not going to be caught out again. Dottie ran as fast as her little legs could take her. Although she felt frightened by this eerie, foggy, dismal place, she did not allow that fear to overwhelm her, and knew her place was with The Goodness.

She really missed her home; she even began to think that Viola was not as mean as she had previously thought compared to the bad influences of this place. No, she knew in her heart that this kind of existence was not for her, she never wanted to be part of it, and she really needed to get out of it.

The voices were everywhere, all getting louder and louder, trying to compete with each other to be heard first so that they could rise out of their wet and muddy graves. "They wouldn't be in here but for the fact of doing such bad things and that they only wanted to get back to doing worse things if their calls were answered," she reassured herself. She knew she had to remain strong, so strong in fact that she was running faster than she ever thought she could. Soon, with repeated attempts, she was finally far enough from Mai's influence to be able to summon her Cheromaack back to her, she never felt so relieved to hear it swoosh down to her.

She felt so happy to have it around her again and to feel so protected. Now, once more, she was able to fly freely.

Mai and Mani were furious that she had managed to give them the slip and outwitted them—Mai was now in hot pursuit. A race had started in the skies and Dottie was leading. She kept soaring up and dipping down, feeling glad that all her training going down the stairs on her family's silver tray was now coming in handy. She would soar vertically up away from Mai, she was able to leave her for dust as she descended at a phenomenal speed away from her. Mai's flying style was too conservative, and Mani was grounded as would never make a skilled aviator, Curlocks were rudimentary beings. Dottie was able to keep abreast of Mai using all the techniques she had learned herself; Dottie couldn't help feeling very proud of herself for getting away from her nasty clutches.

Nell was going to be so proud of her she thought to herself, but then, suddenly, her Cheromaack felt heavy and unresponsive, her flying became leaden as if somehow her magic cloak was being controlled by someone else. Against her best efforts her flight slowed and slowly she floated down to the ground once again. Once landed Dottie was surrounded, she was caught,

"Oh-Oh!" she said. Mai had caught her in another of her devious traps.

"Did you really think you could escape me, my girl? NOW Mani, take her to Neslock, and I will deal with her there.

"Let me go you beast, let me go," Dottie said, as she tried to wriggle out of his clutches, but he just laughed.

"You could really hurt a fella's feelings with them words, now you can just shut up," he yelled.

Mani grabbed both of little Dottie's arms and lifted her clear off the ground. He was about to shake her angrily, when suddenly an intensely bright light blinded him. He screamed in pain; dropping Dottie as he desperately tried to hide from this searing light. It was The Goodness.

"Oh, good boy, good boy, just in the nick of time," said Dottie with delight.

Both Mai and her minion were dazzled by the light of The Goodness, Dottie once more had full control of her Cheromaack, and flew over and stood behind him as he dealt with the nasty duo. Mai screamed, her whole body contorted, and she scurried away into the distance. She knew she had only a moment to escape from that intense light before it cleansed her completely, and she would forget all her dastardly ways, and for a time, end up a simpering wreck like Sherida. Mani curled up into a sorrowful ball bemoaning his faith; Curlocks you see do not become cleansed by the light but merely suffer its after-effects for a season or two.

"OH Goodness, I knew you would save me," said a grateful Dottie. "I nearly got away from them but then suddenly they trapped me, try as I might I just could not get my Cheromaack under my full control. I felt sick to my stomach at the thought that I was going to have to live out the rest of my life doing their bidding." She hugged him and bathed in his bright soothing light; the glow made her feel so good that she could achieve anything.

Dottie explained to The Goodness how they were able to kidnap her, and she explained in detail all their malicious plans with the Underearthers. They both knew they had an arduous task ahead; to rescue Nell and Juni. The Goodness flew high into the sky to gain a better perspective on their situation. Far in the distance he could make out a disturbance over the city where Mai had fled back to. He looked to Dottie, and she could tell by the serious look in his eyes, this was where they must go to, into the heart of the bad.

CHAPTER 39

The Student Becomes the Master

As they flew toward the charred remains of the city, they could make out a vortex in the sky dead ahead. Two hapless beings were held within it being tossed around like feathers in the wind.

"Oh no, NO....it's Nell and Juni, Goodness...can you see?!" Nell and Juni were caught up in the ferocious whirlwind, it was such a violent storm, twisting and turning. Dottie saw that the two sorcerers were completely trapped. She instinctively knew what she had to do, and like all heroes, she acted without hesitation. She was fearless and flew up from The Goodness's back to launch her own mini whirlwind to counter the vortex. Dottie rose up, high above it, to unravel it, by flying in the opposite direction to the vortex's rotation, flying round and round in an effort to slow its vicious spinning. The Goodness was now growing ever stronger and brighter and, in doing so, the dark vortex began to struggle, and then weaken, in his proximity. Nell and Juni averted their eyes as they knew what was coming; suddenly The Goodness climbed high into the air, just over the top of the vortex then he dived down deep into its core. For a moment, all became dark. Dottie too, flew high up over the top, paused for one moment, as if steeling herself for what lay ahead, then followed The Goodness into the heart of the storm. Nell, Juni, Dottie, and The Goodness, were now completely caught up in Mai's deadly vortex, her trap was sprung.

Inside the swirling storm, all their Cheromaacks were completely disabled, fell off their shoulders and were tossed around, lifeless, and unable to function. The Goodness was bound by his obligation to never cause harm to a member of the C.O.R. He could not directly turn his full power on Mai, who, despite all her wickedness, was still a member of the C.O.R. So, he too was rendered incapacitated by the spinning of this vicious vortex. The maelstrom left him whinnying in fear for the fate of his friends.

Dottie was in the middle of all this, caught up in this ferocious whirlwind, rendered powerless by it, and all now seemed hopeless.

Mai was laughing manically outside the towering vortex at her apparently inevitable victory.

Within the maelstrom, Dottie suddenly felt a new strength building within her. She was somehow able to create a shield around herself without her Cheromaack; a glowing shield protecting her from the pull of the vortex's powerful winds. Outside, Mai stood on the brink of claiming total victory when suddenly, from out of the vortex, Dottie emerged, totally untouched and untroubled. Mai was shocked but kept manipulating the storm.

"Stay back child, stay back lest I blast you," Mai threatened.

"No you won't," replied Dottie.

"You can't blast me and still keep the others caught in your awful storm." Dottie started to chant a spell and raised her right hand up, then pointed it in Mai's direction.

"Hah!" mocked Mai, "Am I supposed to worry what spell a little urchin like you will cast? If even The Goodness cannot stop me, then what can a mere child do?"

Dottie's face took on a cheeky expression and she responded, "Well, that's because The Goodness is too good to hurt you. Me? Well, even my gran says it....there's a wicked streak in me!"

A powerful white light, similar to The Goodness's, shot out from Dottie's outstretched hand and blasted Mai backwards. In doing so, it revealed Dottie's newfound special powers; she too had the ability to emit the same cleansing light as The Goodness.

Mai was left flat on her backside in a heap. Some smoke emanated from her hair, and out of her ears, with only the last remnants of her wickedness slowly fading within her.

Mai had kept a little bit of good in her to protect her from The Goodness's light, and it almost worked. The Goodness, Nell, and Juni were all from realms where good beings were very good and bad beings were very bad. Mai had used that trace of good in her as a means to prevent The Goodness's power from overwhelming her. But Dottie, being from Blusfloct (Earth), was a little different; you see, Blusfloctians, also known as, human beings, were neither all good nor all bad, but all the shades of both. So, because Dottie was good, but with a little bit of bad, she had the ability to counteract and override Mai's powers. She rendered her helpless and unable to do any more harm. Dottie didn't stop there, she kept blasting Mai backwards and blocked all her powers, Mai, sensing her plan was lost, turned, and retreated swiftly into her castle's keep.

Dottie turned to face the vortex to try to help her friends break free from the grip of that cold north whirlwind. She could feel The Goodness was about to surge all his powers to destroy the vortex from within, she averted her eyes. Suddenly, from within, there was a burst of pure white light. The light broke through the wall of the vortex, tearing it asunder until it was no more than a tiny dust devil, and then it dissipated into nothing.

The Goodness landed next to Dottie, as Nell and Juni dusted themselves down, and started to breathe normally again. The light of The Goodness helped them to fully recover from their ordeal. His light was so powerful that it had dissolved any badness near them, and this cleansing light started to shine out and spread over a vast area.

They knew it would now take years for The Badness to repopulate this location with pure wrongdoing again. The indigenous warrior folk of Sherastnorth, now free from the shackles of The Badness. They had witnessed The Goodness and Dottie save their, once proud, realm. Their actions had given Sherastnorth a chance to recover all that had been lost.

Safe for now, Nell hugged Dottie warmly. She was so proud of what the brave little girl had done.

Nell was still worried about Mai. The Goodness nodded to Nell and knew what they must try and achieve. Nell introduced Dottie to Juni who was now, once again, a very strong and beautiful young woman with long black curly hair. When Dottie looked again at Nell, she too had grown younger and more beautiful, with long blond hair. Nell and Juni had taken the spell of eternal youth, so would never grow old. They had chosen to live as older ladies in disguise.

"Eternal youth isn't always a good thing," Juni told Dottie, "It is one of the reasons why Mai became enamoured with badness, she couldn't deal with the eternity of it all. It can drive people mad, this is what we found out about her, and so we still have The Badness to fight."

They all followed the direction that Mai fled, determined to get her out of Sherastnorth.

Dottie had noticed that, wherever The Goodness walked, he left nature growing behind. All sorts of pretty wildflowers grew in his wake. With every step he took, those dark, tortured, vines would shrivel up and be replaced by wonderful bunches of primroses, forget-me-nots, violets, daisies, and dandelions, leaving a floral pathway in his trail.

On they walked steadfastly towards the city of Neslock, and to Mai's citadel.

.

Saving Mai

The walls of the castle were even grimier than before and colossal in scale; they towered over everything. There were beings crowded around fires inside the buildings on all levels, coughing, and groaning in despair. There was an unbearably bad smell wafting up from the alleyways – the stench of oppression.

When these miserable wretches saw The Goodness approaching, they recoiled, his white light seared into their darkened hearts; they fell away holding their heads screaming. No one could come near him unless they were good. Nell could sense that Mai was hiding inside this grey building directly in front of them, so grey and cold looking as it loomed over them, you could see the tops of the building and all around it was dark and gloomy.

"Why would she want to stay here?" Dottie thought-asked.

"We do not know what happened to her to make her so sure she wanted to live in a place like this. She seems possessed by one of the bad forces in here, that is the only way we can make sense of it all," Juni thought-replied.

"Well, no matter where she goes or what she does we are just going to have to barge in there, and take her back, whether she likes it or not," Nell said in a determined fashion.

In they went and forced open the large wooden double doors. The doors sprang open, both halves slammed hard with an almighty bang against the stone walls. Mai was seeking her escape—she was flying high above them when they entered, screaming out with manic laughter as she flew past, sneering down at them.

"What do you think you are doing here? This is MY sanctum, begone you hags!" She dived and darted, but Nell and Juni had every escape route blocked. Mai fumed, "You are both so pathetic," she roared out loudly, as she swooped past them. "You think you can cure me, do you?? Hah – you can think again, you are nothing to me – do you hear – NOTHING! The future is with me and my ways, my people are here, my peers are living here, you have nothing I want, do you hear me?!" she screamed at the top of her voice.

Nell and Juni were moving in, closer and closer, sealing off any chance Mai had of escaping. She was cornered. Without her realising, they had placed a gentle binding spell on Mai, making it impossible for her to leave that room, until they lifted the spell. "You are changing Mai; can you feel it? Nell asked, smiling and in a gentle voice. Even now, before their eyes they could see the effect her recent exposure to The Goodness' light was having on their old friend.

Mai had known she would have to keep a bit of good in her in order to have any chance of resisting The Goodness. This was her secret, as she was able to get nearer to him than any of the other bad practitioners. Her plan was to try and use this trace of goodness to shield herself from his powers and maybe, somehow, transmit some of The Badness into him, to weaken him perhaps, and ultimately take control of him. Her plan worked up to a point, in that she was able to stay near him, but she had completely underestimated his powers, and now Dottie's too.

She mistook goodness for weakness, and the closer she got to The Goodness, the brighter he shone. Mai had inadvertently triggered the inoculation of her own being from the powers of The Badness. One exposure to his light was all it took to effect a cure. The closer she got, step-by-step; the less and less of The Badness could remain in her.

"Look at yourself Mai, you are turning back," Nell shouted. "You old crone, don't be ridiculous, that is never going to happen to me," she roared. Mai attempted to conjure another vortex, to ensnare Nell and Juni once more, but her power was diminishing. She landed on the ground and came eye to-eye with Nell. Both now stood face-to-face. Nell spoke softly now, pointing in the direction of the ornate wall mirror,

"Take a look Mai, look at yourself, your eyes are returning to their natural blue colour."

"No, NO, nooo, they are NOT! They are never going back, and she sped off using what was left of her bad powers to break the binding spell and made good her escape. Nell grabbed the mirror of the wall and pursued Mai. Using magic, they could track her no matter where she tried to hide. They followed her into another room in the castle; she was now seated at a wooden table.

"She keeps responding to the Underearthers' call, that is why she is stuck in here," Nell observed.

"Stop the light, that light is burning me, I can't take it anymore, stop it, it is destroying me, ST'TOOPP!!!" she cried out piteously. Mai was in agony, and she held her head in her hands screaming out for it to stop.

"The Goodness is with us, so she cannot bear being exposed to his cleansing light," Nell said. Mai was the only resident of Sherastnorth who could withstand his light for any length of time; there was still a trace of her better nature buried deep inside her. However, her bad side, while sorely weakened now, still caused her body to recoil and twist from The Goodness's power.

"Mai has just been possessed by those who dwell here, she is doing their bidding, look how weakened she is now, and I can see that she was still good underneath all her wickedness," Juni remarked to Nell. Nell agreed, and then, turning her full attention onto Mai said in a calm commanding voice,

"You are changing back Mai – we can see that. "No, NO NOOO!" Mai attempted to fly but she was so weakened now she merely raised a few inches off the ground then fell back down. Nell and Juni seized their opportunity and both women held the ornate mirror up to Mai.

"LOOK!" They both incanted – "LOOK!!!" Mai looked at her reflection and could see her piercing blue eyes staring back at her. Then she noticed her hair was turning from its knotted, greying, and dry frizzled state, back to its natural glossy raven black. Her skin too was smooth with a glowing light emanating from it, and her hands were no longer gnarled. She could see the change and started shouting,

"NO, NO, NOO!! This cannot be happening." "No No No!!!" She covered her face with her hands, and she slumped into a heap on the floor sobbing uncontrollably.

"Quickly Juni—let's grab her and pull her out of the room while we have this advantage now over The Badness."

Nell and Juni each took Mai by her arms and flew her as far away as possible to weaken its dark hold over her. They knew that just by that brief exposure to The Goodness' light Mai would no longer be able to resist. Its healing power had permeated deep into her core and had started to usurp the negative energies that had held her captive. Nell wrapped her cloak partially around her while they all travelled upwards into the grey sky.

"The Goodness is shining a bright light near us, all of us will be able to fly well out of this place now and to safety," Nell shouted to the others.

"Yes, the further we get away from The Badness, the weaker Mai is going to get," said Juni with a smile. Mai fainted, finally succumbing to the exhaustion of her internal struggle. They took her back to The Goodness's realm where she could slowly recuperate.

"There is so much Badness back there in Sherastnorth, the only way we can enter that realm from now on, is with The Goodness by our side. Otherwise, we risk danger during The Turning, just as Mai did," Nell explained. "Mai had been our best and see what can happen when we leave our guard down, even for a moment – it's just too dangerous." All nodded in agreement. As Mai came to, she had no memory of all that had occurred, it was as if she had suddenly awoken from a bad dream.

"I'm very confused, why am I here? Nell, Juni, old friends, what are you two doing here? I haven't seen you both in ages, how lovely. Where have you been? Is there to be a party? I have not even had a moment to do my hair, and why am I wearing such an awful tatty old dress?" Mai asked, confused by it all. Everyone looked at each other for a moment and broke down in laughter.

"We have a lot of explaining to do don't we girls?" Nell said, giggling and hugging Dottie. Nell then warmly hugged Mai and Juni and she let them catch up. The Goodness nudged Dottie and she just giggled with delight. They were all so happy that everyone was back safe and sound. "A party you say?" said Nell, "Why not, why not indeed!" And with a waving of her hands a delightful afternoon tea materialised for all to enjoy. Nell even remembered some sweet carrots for The Goodness to munch on. As the evening wore on the old friends and the young sorceress laughed and joked and shared happy hours in each other's company.

CHAPTER 41

Epilogue

Nell and Dottie said their goodbyes to the battle-weary friends before leaving the tea party and heading back to Blusfloct. Once back at Nell's cottage, Dottie set about building a fire and filling the old black kettle with water to set upon the stove. As she did so, Dottie hummed a tune the fairies had thought her. Nell watched Dottie back being a helpful little girl again. It pleased the old tutor immensely to see that her student remained so unspoiled, and unaffected, by all she had encountered.

"I chose well," Nell, thought to herself, "such ability and fearlessness cannot be taught, it was latent in this girl from the moment she was born. Her gift is truly astounding."

"I can hear what you are thinking you know," thought Dottie. Nell laughed aloud.

"Oh, silly me, I forgot you have that gift now too," thought-spoke Nell. "I am very impressed with your progress Dottie." Nell was so proud of how far her little student had come since that very first day they began her training. After a time, the stove was fully aflame, and Nell made a pot of cocoa for herself and Dottie. She poured it into two large daintily decorative porcelain cups for each of them, leaving the remainder warming on the stove for top ups. In the distance they could hear Dottie's mother calling her,

"Dottie....DOTTIE....your tea's ready...come along now before it gets cold."

Nell took Dottie's hand in hers, as they walked down the pathway of the cottage, then up along the short lane until just at the gate of Dottie's house. "You see, I told you I'd have you home in time for your tea," Nell said with a wink.

And so, did Dottie's magical gifts and fantastical adventures change her home life back on Mount Garra farm? No, not one little bit. Gran continued to be Gran, pandering to Viola's every need, and always suspicious that Dottie was up to mischief, but never sure what exactly that mischief was. Viola continued to be a mean older sister and always in a grump about something and nothing.

What had changed however, was Dottie; Viola's tantrums no longer bothered her nor did her gran's reprimands, in fact, she found both to be comforting in their own ways – far less daunting than an argumentative trenic, a scheming curlock or a whirligig witch.

THE END

Printed in Great Britain
by Amazon

31125976R00116